SMITTEN BY MAGIC

MAGIC & MAYHEM #3

ERICA RIDLEY

A previous edition was published as *Midwinter Magic*.

ALSO BY ERICA RIDLEY

Magic & Mayhem:

Kissed by Magic

Must Love Magic

Smitten by Magic

Gothic Love Stories:

Too Wicked to Kiss

Too Sinful to Deny

Too Tempting to Resist

Too Wanton to Wed

Rogues to Riches:

Lord of Chance

Lord of Pleasure

Lord of Night

Lord of Temptation

Lord of Secrets

Lord of Vice

Dukes of War:

The Viscount's Tempting Minx

The Earl's Defiant Wallflower

The Captain's Bluestocking Mistress

The Major's Faux Fiancée
The Brigadier's Runaway Bride
The Pirate's Tempting Stowaway
The Duke's Accidental Wife

The 12 Dukes of Christmas:

Once Upon a Duke
Kiss of a Duke
Wish Upon a Duke
Never Say Duke
Dukes, Actually
The Duke's Bride
The Duke's Embrace
The Duke's Desire
Dawn With a Duke
One Night With a Duke
Ten Days With a Duke
Forever Your Duke

CHAPTER 1

Javier Rodriguez swung his heavy burlap sacks off the back of the stranger's pickup truck. He leapt over the tailgate and grunted when his Gore-Tex hiking boots landed hard on the cracked asphalt. He tried to offer cash to the sun-worn family stuffed into the truck's cab, but they waved off the money, waved him off, too, and continued toward the mountains, a stream of exhaust smoke trailing in their wake. Javier hiked his sacks back onto his aching shoulders and hauled himself up the two-kilometer stretch into town.

Santita, Bolivia. Population: Six hundred. Amenities: Scarce. Not most CEOs' idea of a luxury Christmas vacation, but then again, Javier had given up on both "luxury" and "vacation" when he'd walked out of last month's congressional hearing a free man. The government would pen new statutes to better guide industry practices in the future, but nothing could be done about the past. After all, no laws had been broken. Any exploited resources had been depleted legally. He and his Fortune 500 counterparts were free to retire with billions of dollars and a clean slate.

Javier's conscience disagreed.

He'd thought purchasing "carbon offset" land in rural Bolivia where his great-grandparents had been born would be enough. Protecting his ancestral land and sharing a portion of his money in one set-it-and-forget-it dash of his signature across the bottom of a page. He'd let himself believe that one good deed canceled out all the rest. After all, his mission wasn't philanthropy.

It was profit. And he was a media darling.

No businessman made the cover of *Time* magazine without ruthless ambition and relentless momentum. But his face on the cover had impacted him far less than the gut-punch of images shown during the hearing. The true cost of being a so-called "unicorn" startup wasn't eighty-hour work weeks and a drawer full of antacids. Every penny of their success had ruined someone else's quality of life.

While his ex-partners congratulated themselves on becoming filthy rich before the government could stop them, Javier had simply felt filthy. His eyes had been opened, and he would never again value a conglomerate over an individual. No more impersonal signatures on contracts.

It was time to walk the walk.

And so here he was, at the crossroads of the Andes Mountains and the Bolivian lowlands, making his own penance for the damage his industry had wrought.

Or trying to, anyway. Getting out of California had taken nearly three weeks.

Heading *toward* his Malibu beach house was never a big deal. Limos and private jets were as easy to score as pumpkin spice lattes. But leaving the States for a remote dot in the rainforest—or going anywhere without artisanal tater tots and 5G networks—was all but impossible. Even for him. It was as if a forcefield of Murphy's Law intended to trap him inside the 90625 zip code.

As quickly as he made airline reservations, his flights got canceled without notification. Uber Black chauffeurs suffered flat tires just pulling out of his driveway. LAX customs officials grilled him about his crates full of toys and medicine and children's clothing until he missed every possible flight and had to start all over the next morning.

Once he managed to get on a plane, mechanical failure or missing flight crew kept it grounded. When the plane finally took off and reached cruising altitude, inclement weather diverted him first to Vegas and then to Aspen. When he landed at his actual destination, immigration officials warned him of malaria and dengue and avian flu and offered to send him right back home, free of charge.

The moment he refused this largesse, the wheels and zippers of his sturdy, custom-made luggage spontaneously fell apart, strewing crayons and penicillin along the baggage belts. When he rejected the reiterated offer of a free return to Malibu in favor of stuffing whatever he could salvage into discarded burlap sacks that still carried the faint scent of coffee beans, the car rental company he'd hired as well as the backup car rental company he'd also hired and every other car rental company in Bolivia were inexplicably fresh out of drivers and vehicles.

Which was how Javier Rodriguez, ex-Fortune 500 leading man, found himself sharing a truck bed with four skinny goats for the 185 mostly-paved kilometers between the Sucre airport and the rural chili town of Padilla, his luggage reduced to dirt-stained burlap sacks… and if he wasn't careful, even less than that. Who knew goats ate burlap? And crayons?

It would've been much easier to give up and go home. But Javier hadn't taken his company from fledgling startup to international powerhouse in ten short years by being the sort who gave up and went home.

Plus, it was already December. Only a few weeks until Christmas. And he'd promised the children of Santita that, this year, *Noche Buena* would truly be a good one.

He stumbled downhill, a couple hundred yards from the spare room he'd coaxed from the town dentist—all traditional lodging had naturally been unable to accommodate his request.

Suddenly, he smacked into an invisible wall.

Everything went flying, including him. Giant snow-white wings and a blinding light filled his vision and vanished just as quickly.

Javier landed on his ass and blinked in befuddlement at the empty space in front of him. Maybe it wasn't a brick wall after all... but it was equally as mystifying.

He could've sworn he'd run into another person—someone swathed in a gangster-huge fur coat. Something soft and wide and hairy and completely unnecessary in sixty-five-degree weather. The breeze had a nip to it, sure, but head-to-toe fur was a bit much. Only a crazy person tromped around Bolivia dressed like a Sasquatch.

But no one was there. Just an empty gravel road, littered with coloring books and chewable vitamins and a dazed and confused ex-CEO.

Maybe *he* was the crazy person.

With a muttered curse, he started stuffing his donation supplies back into the burlap sacks for what felt like the millionth time that day. Every single muscle ached. He was hungry and exhausted and no doubt hallucinating from stress and sleep deprivation. There'd been no enormous white wings, no '20s gangster wrapped in snow-bleached fur, no—

Clipboard.

There was a clipboard on the road, half-hidden beneath one of the comic books that had fallen from his stack. He jerked his head up and scanned all sides of the empty road. A few goats, several chickens, plenty of gravel, but no sign of anyone who might've dropped a clipboard in his path.

Except whomever he'd run into.

The clipboard couldn't have been there long. For one thing, the clipboard wasn't dirty—and anything lying on a dirt road for more than a few seconds got very, very dirty. Javier could well imagine the current state of his backside.

Also present beneath the fallen clipboard were a handful of mismatched Barbie shoes and a Hot Wheels car, further confirming the clip-board had fallen at the same time he had. But from where? From whom?

He looked around slowly, carefully, every sense on high alert. But this was rural Latin America on a Sunday evening. The only thing open was the church. Every townsperson was either inside their homes eating dinner or attending Sunday mass. More importantly, he was in the middle of a large open area. There wasn't even anywhere to *hide,* not as quickly as the accident had happened.

Except here he was, dusting off jump ropes and children's tennis shoes, right next to a clip-board that Should Not Be.

Once he got his precious donations re-secured in the burlap sacks, he picked up the clipboard for a closer look.

~~Malibu~~

~~Los Angeles~~
~~Houston~~
~~La Paz~~
~~Sucre~~
Santita

His itinerary. Javier's stomach dropped. He was dehydrated and bone-weary and wound so tight he could snap, but he wasn't hallucinating. Someone had a copy of his travel itinerary, stop for stop. Someone was *following* him. Or had arrived first in anticipation.

But who? And how? And why?

He looked around again, slowly, carefully, his farcical bad luck now taking on a sinister edge. He sat on his haunches in the middle of the empty road, ready to spring up at a moment's notice.

When he'd dissolved his corporation, he'd given every employee an extraordinarily handsome severance package, from the legal team through the janitorial crew, so there was no cause for concern on that front. That documentary on the far-reaching impacts of corporate greed still ran on late-night TV, but it vilified soulless conglomerates in general, not him specifically.

And yet... Javier's fingers gripped the clipboard, smudging the pristine page with his dusty fingerprints. And *yet.*

He leapt to his feet.

"I know you're out there!" he shouted into the evening wind, raising the clipboard over his head like Lloyd Dobler's boombox in *Say Anything*.

Javier's *abuelos* had ensured he'd grown up speaking Spanish, but for now he stuck with English. Whoever wrote this list had started in Malibu. He was probably a gringo—and possibly as ruthless as Javier himself.

"Come out, come out, whoever you are," he called, his voice singsong and infused with anger. He didn't like mysteries, and he especially despised any situation that made him look foolish. Such as yelling his head off in front of a goat and a few chickens. "Show yourself right this second, or so help me—"

A woman stepped out of the shadows.

Presumably the shadows, anyway. Purple sky shot with pink from the setting sun did tend to lower visibility, but he could swear the spindly trees dotting along the road weren't nearly thick enough to hide a person.

And yet here she was. His mystery stalker. Looking less terrifying than he'd imagined, and more... terrified. Good. She ought to be scared.

He, for one, was speechless.

She had bright hazel eyes, a pert little nose, bronze skin, and golden-blonde Shirley Temple ringlets... which might not have seemed out of place on, say, an eight-year-old girl instead of what appeared to be a twenty-eight-year-old woman. She stood about average height—maybe a head shorter than Javier himself—but there was nothing else average about her. She wore a gold-and-purple Lakers jersey over the neon green straps of a string bikini top, calf-length rainbow-striped yoga pants, mind-blowingly impractical stiletto-heeled sandals with white powder puffs, and a plastic headband with a hot pink cupcake sticking out of it.

His niece had a headband just like it.

His niece was seven.

This woman... Javier shook his head to clear it. It didn't help. He tried to think logically, which would've been much easier had there been anything logical at all about the woman before him. She looked like she'd gotten her getup from some Halloween costume labeled "California Girl." The kind sold on Mars. For the extraterrestrial tourist who wants to blend with the earthlings.

If this was a stalker, he'd eat the clipboard.

"Who *are* you?" he managed to get out, once his throat started working.

"Sarah," she answered automatically, her voice low and strangely melodious. "Sarah Phimm."

He choked in disbelief. "Sarah Phimm? Seriously? Well, I'm 'No Way José.'"

She stared at him in cherubic innocence, as if she hadn't gotten the joke.

Forget it. He held up the clipboard. "What are you doing with my itinerary, Sarah Phimm?"

"It's *my* itinerary."

He didn't bother to hide his skepticism. The woman was wearing a cupcake. On her head. "*You're* from Malibu?"

"I came from there this morning," she said, which didn't precisely answer the question. "Anybody arriving from Malibu has that itinerary. It's either that, or layover in Miami. And Miami is, you know... *Miami*."

Javier happened to *like* Miami. Most of his family lived there. Then again, who knew where this lady had been hatched?

He narrowed his eyes, trying to picture a world in which it was okay to take someone in a cupcake headband seriously. He wasn't even sure he could take *himself* seriously at this point. Think. He rubbed his temples. Okay. So she flew in from LAX. That still didn't explain her My First Earthling getup—or why some *loca* with time and money on her hands would choose a remote Bolivian village, of all destinations.

"Why here?" he demanded. "Why come to Santita?"

"Why not?" she countered with a little shrug. "You're here, aren't you?"

He frowned. Not at her logic, which was incredibly flawed, but because when she'd lifted her shoulder, a soft rustling accompanied the movement, like spring leaves fluttering in an afternoon breeze.

There were plenty of leafy trees and brisk winds here in Santita, but neither should be coming from the direction of Sarah Phimm's shoulders.

He had to be more sleep-deprived than he'd thought.

She held out her hand. "Can I help with the bags?"

"No." Javier handed back her clipboard, then hiked the burlap sacks back up over his bruised shoulders.

Every muscle screamed in protest. He ignored the pain. He might be dead tired, but the contents of those bags were his responsibility. The well-stocked replacement shipping containers he'd ordered wouldn't arrive until January. After the frustrating three-week adventure getting back to Bolivia from California, there was no way he'd risk jaunting home again before Christmas for another shopping spree.

Ignoring the strange woman, he resumed his laborious trek toward the dentist's house.

She fell in beside him. "Where are you going?"

He glanced over at her, his lips shut tight. He suspected she knew precisely where he was headed. He decided to turn the tables. "Where are *you* going?"

"Oh, you know..." She waved her hand in the general direction of nowhere. "Around."

That was precious. Did she not want to name a hotel because she worried he might spy on *her?* She clearly wasn't from around here. In a town this small, people recognized each other's chickens on sight. Everyone from the local seamstress to the kid who ran the vegetable stand probably knew where she was staying.

And her real name.

He tightened his grip on the heavy sacks and turned the corner toward the dentist's house. Thinking about vegetable stands had reminded him just how hungry he was—and how there'd be nothing for him to eat. The dentist and his wife would be down at mass. There might be food in their kitchen, but although Javier could replace anything he ate after the supermarket opened the next day, he couldn't risk inadvertently consuming something his hosts intended to have for their evening meal.

"Damn," he muttered.

"What?"

He thunked the burlap sacks onto the front porch between a hammock and a worn rocking chair. Sarah was two steps behind him—and didn't appear to be in a hurry to leave.

"Don't suppose you know someplace open for dinner?" he asked sarcastically.

"Uhh..." Her eyelashes fluttered. Not flirtatiously... more like in intense concentration. Or like she was about to have a *petit mal* seizure.

Just when he started to get concerned, her hazel eyes sprang back open. “Sure. I know a place.”

He narrowed his own eyes to slits. She did *not* know a place. There was no place to know. He’d just left here three weeks ago—returning home had been surprisingly easy—and he could attest to the complete lack of Sunday evening dining options. But his stomach was growling, he was desperate, and she was certainly intriguing, to say the least. And oddly fetching, despite—or perhaps because of—the jaunty pink cupcake protruding from her hair.

“Okay,” he said with a sigh. “I’ll bite.”

She took a hurried step back, eyes wide. *“Me?”*

He gaped at her, momentarily speechless. Maybe English wasn’t her first language after all. “Not *you*. ‘I’ll bite’ just means go ahead and show me the restaurant you’re talking about. If it exists, I’ll buy you dinner.”

Her eyes did the fluttering thing again. Then she said, “Sure.”

One simple word. *Sure*. But her expression was unnerving. She beamed at him with an alarming level of Internet-meme-quality enthusiasm. Her smile too wide, her teeth too sparkly, her hazel eyes... unearthly. The back of Javier’s neck tingled.

He should’ve gone to bed hungry.

CHAPTER 2

Sarah's fingers trembled as Javier swung open the door to the cozy cement-block house and lugged his heavy sacks inside. Scratch that. Not just her fingers. Her knees trembled, her shoulders trembled, every invisible feather upon her wings trembled.

He was *not supposed to see her*. Under any circumstances.

But what was she supposed to do? He'd known she was there, even before he could see her. He'd run right into her, with enough force to crack the clipboard against her nose. It still stung. But not as badly as her punishment if her superiors ever found out.

Technically, she'd run into Javier, not the other way around. He had the excuse of not being able to see her. Sarah had the bad habit of looking at her cursed clipboard instead of watching him, as she was contractually obligated to do.

Not that staring at him was a burden. Javier Rodriguez was divine.

Well, not *divine*-divine. He was one hundred percent human, which made him very off-limits. But he was the perfect combination of wavy black hair and warm brown eyes and six feet of lean muscle that, for most of his adult life, had either been gift-wrapped in no-nonsense business suits or dripping with sweat at his private gym.

So, yeah. Not exactly a big sacrifice to keep her eyes on him at all times.

And she would've, if it hadn't been for that damn clipboard. Her one vice. Well, second if you counted ogling her client. And maybe third, if you counted saying "damn."

She was a guardian angel. Specifically, Javier Rodriguez's guardian angel. And she would've remained his very secret, very *invisible* heaven-approved bodyguard, if she'd been staring at him instead of at her clipboard.

Being an angel, she didn't need clipboards, or mortal crutches of any kind. But it wasn't about what she needed. She *liked* lists. Even if every word was already committed to her perfect recall, there was just something satisfying about striking out each completed line item, of gazing at a long tidy row with more tasks complete than incomplete.

Especially in this case, where she was actively trying to prevent her client from continuing to the next item. His well-being was her responsibility. California was safe. Amazonian rain forests were not.

But Javier Rodriguez was the most stubborn, ambitious, ruthlessly determined human Sarah had ever dealt with. And although he was driving her to an early grave—or would be, if angels weren't virtually immortal—she might have an eensy weensy crush on all that strong, focused determination.

She'd never given her feelings more thought than that. There was no point. He was human, she wasn't. She was invisible, he wasn't. Interaction was so not even a remote possibility, as to almost preclude the fantasy.

Until now.

Once he'd seen that clipboard—and had a brief glimpse of her true self in the process—she'd had to materialize, to protect his human psyche. It would look extremely unfavorable on her end-of-month review should it come to light she'd inadvertently driven insane the very person she was assigned to protect.

Now it was just a matter of waiting for an opportune moment to disappear. She'd planned to vanish as soon as he stepped inside the dentist's house—when he emerged to find her gone, he'd assume she was the lunatic, not him—but all he did was shove the worn sacks inside the door and turn back around with an expectant look on his dangerously handsome face.

She felt bad about being responsible for the crappy sacks. And the luggage. And the rental cars. And the planes. She'd just wanted him to stay home. Stay *safe*. But he made it so damn hard.

The conditions of her employment specifically stated that her magic—pardon, her "miracles," although Javier might not see them that way—could only affect the assigned party. She'd gone into a gray area when she'd diverted his first plane to Vegas, although she'd ensured that the other passengers had been rebooked on alternate flights. She'd thrown everything at him she could think of to keep him in the world he knew, but Javier Rodriguez hadn't become the man he was today by being easy to push around.

And now she owed him dinner.

He gestured toward the dirt road. "Well?"

Sarah gulped. He wasn't smiling at her. He rarely smiled at anyone anymore, which was a huge waste if you asked her. His smile was breathtaking. Right now, though, he was tired and hungry, both of which were her fault.

"This way." She hopped off the front stoop and headed toward the road.

When he didn't immediately follow, she froze in horror.

Had she hopped off the stoop? Or had she, maybe, *floated* off the stoop out of habit? Good Lord, pretending to be human was hard.

She snuck a glance over her shoulder.

His eyes were dark, unreadable. But he stepped off the stoop with a shake of his head and fell in beside her.

"Where are we headed?" he asked. But as soon as they rounded the first corner, awareness registered on his face. "Doña Camila? She's not open on Sundays."

Sarah didn't answer. Partly because she wasn't used to answering aloud—conversational skills tended to deteriorate when you spent your life as someone's invisible shadow—but mostly she didn't answer because he was right, and he was wrong.

Doña Camila ran a small restaurant attached to her home. She wasn't open on Sundays because that was when her son dropped off the grandkids, but he and his wife had miraculously stumbled across a four-pack of tickets to a rodeo they hadn't even known was scheduled for tonight. Because Sarah had just invented it. Which meant Doña Camila had no particular plans for the evening, outside of fixing dinner for any stray walk-ins who happened to be about.

Javier's pace quickened as soon as he caught sight of the older woman sitting out front in her wood-and-leather rocking chair.

She greeted them with a smile, and bid them to take any seat they chose. The restaurant layout was typical for the area—small, open, nothing more than a simple pitched roof atop rustic wooden columns, with a tiny kitchen tucked in the back, where Doña Camila did all the cooking. The few tables were preset with laminated menus and silverware wrapped in white paper napkins. Since there were no walls, every seat had a great view.

Javier picked a table up in front, with the best breeze and a splendid vista of the mountains. Sarah eased into the chair across from him, careful to mind her wings. When Doña Camila came to take their order, Javier gestured for Sarah to choose first.

"You go ahead." She pushed her menu away. "I already ate."

She hadn't eaten, of course. Ever. In her life. And as much as she'd like to taste human food, now that she was visible and could actually have some, she wasn't really sure what would happen if she tried. Was human food suitable for angel metabolisms? Did angels even *have* metabolisms?

Wait... her boss's daughter was only half-angel, and *she* could eat human food without ill-effect. Then again, this wasn't the moment for Sarah to discover that her belly didn't react the same way.

Javier gave her a long, hard look, then ordered his meal in flawless Spanish, right down to the accent.

Everything he did was flawless. He'd been early to walk, early to read, early to college, and early to become CEO of a multibillion-dollar enterprise. None of which had anything to do with Sarah.

Her job was limited to keeping him safe, not keeping him rich or powerful or successful. Just safe. How he spent the rest of his life was up to him. It would be so much easier on both sides if he would just stop choosing to spend his time barreling headfirst into reckless, risky adventures.

Javier's scheduled coronary wasn't slated until the week after his seventieth birthday, but it had been tough as hell even getting him halfway there. The man was fearless. He knew no boundaries, no limitations. If he wanted to manipulate a controlling share of the U.S. economy, then so be it. If he wanted to go traipsing through the Amazon, outrunning dengue mosquitos and sloshing knee-deep in nonpotable water, then by God, he would. And Sarah would do her best to keep him safe while he did so. She had to. It was going to be hard enough to lose him when he turned seventy. There was no way she'd let him go early.

She fidgeted with her napkin and tried not to overtly stare while he enjoyed his meal. Thirty-five years she'd been watching over him. Watching him ride a bicycle, pledge a fraternity, pilot an airplane. She'd seen him through sickness and through health, through the birth of his niece and the death of his father, through a string of unhappy relationships and many lonely nights, closing his eyes in a Parisian or London or Bangkok penthouse between whirlwind meetings. She'd laughed with him, cried with him, wanted to throw people against a wall with him, stood right by his side in every venture he'd ever made...

And, until now, he'd never even known she existed.

She set down her napkin and stifled a sigh. Face it. He *still* didn't know she existed. Not the real Sarah, the one who squealed over every triumph and wept over every loss, knowing every setback would only make him try harder.

All Javier saw was a pretend Sarah. An amalgamation of ideal memories, conjured automatically without a microsecond's thought. She was almost as surprised as he had been at the outcome.

Her face and hair and eyes and body—all that was the real Sarah. Minus the wings. But she'd wrapped herself beneath the disguise of past happy moments. From his life, of course. Guardian angels didn't have many moments of their own, so she'd subconsciously appropriated his.

The jersey was easy to figure out. Javier was a Lakers super-fan. He had front-row season tickets and recorded the games to watch again later. He had the entire franchise memorized. When they became the first team in NBA history to win three thousand regular season games, Javier had bought a round of drinks for the whole stadium. The crowd had gone wild.

The yoga pants, on the other hand, had nothing to do with the Lakers. Those probably came from a conversation Javier had had with his financial advisor on the private terrace of a trendy Malibu bar. A handful of women had walked by in crop tops and yoga pants, and the men had commented that the government really ought to make a law stating that if you had the body for yoga pants, it was a crime not to wear them. (A similar comment had been made about Brazilian-style bikinis.)

The stiletto sandals were life-endangering on downhill gravel roads, and Sarah well knew where *they* came from. She'd been there when Javier had bought them for his ex-girlfriend. Before she was an ex, of course. That day, he'd told her she'd make him the happiest man alive if she wore the stilettos for him that evening in bed. And maybe he was... for a few hours. The happiness ended when he discovered she was on his rival's payroll, and he had been nothing more than an assignment. Seduce, spy, steal.

Sarah swallowed. For her, this wasn't just an assignment. Even though, contractually, that's what it was supposed to be. But how could anyone spend thirty-five years with someone as amazing as Javier Rodriguez, and not develop feelings?

That was why she had a fuchsia cupcake fascinator sticking out of her head. He'd bought one for his niece on her first trip to Disneyland, and told the little girl that she was what made it the most magical place on Earth. When she'd giggled delightedly and thrown herself into his arms, Javier had grinned—and held on tight.

That was eight long months ago, and the last time Sarah had seen him smile. She wished she could give that moment back to him, over and over, for the rest of his life. He deserved some happiness. He was a good man, no matter what he believed. He had a *destiny*. Sarah's job was to ensure he lived long enough to fulfill it.

Right now, he was looking at her as if he believed her to be no better than the original owner of the white-puff stilettos. Perhaps those hadn't been the wisest choice. His suspicious expression indicated he was already plotting how to force her to give up her secrets. She couldn't let that happen.

Which meant she had to end this charade, stat. She couldn't simply disappear when he wasn't looking, however. Not now. Javier was too focused, too analytical, too... *relentless* to let something like that go. Where would a single woman without visible transportation disappear to in the middle of nowhere? Whether he believed her to be a spy, or whether he just hated mysteries, he wouldn't rest until he found her. Not if he thought it possible she might be in need of rescue.

And try explaining, "I accidentally became my human assignment's primary obsession" to the Governing Council of Heavenly Beings. No, thank you. They couldn't take her wings—she'd been born with them—but they could, and would, take her position away. She'd be demoted from a guardian angel to tooth fairy quicker than she could blink.

Whatever story she was going to come up with, she had to come up with it fast. He was on his last bite of food. Any second now, he was going to expect... conversation.

Sarah's throat dried at the thought. Conversation. With Javier Rodriguez. Alone together in an otherwise empty restaurant, with the Andes mountain range before them and the purple sunset all around. Cozy. Beautiful. Romantic. She swallowed. Was this what it would feel like to be on a date? Her heartbeat sped up. She hadn't been this nervous since she'd first spread her wings.

Javier had become incredibly appealing and incredibly awesome and incredibly not even an option. She'd always acknowledged his toe-curling hotness in much the same way human women acknowledged a half-hearted crush on Idris Elba or Channing Tatum. In an alternate universe where stranger things could happen? Sure. But that wasn't the universe they lived in.

At least, it hadn't been. She'd never become corporeal in front of any of her clients before. Never even dreamed about it, until Javier. And now here they were. In the flesh. Staring at each other across a candlelit table. Like a tongue-tied couple on their first date.

It's not a date, Sarah reminded herself fiercely. *It's not a date. It's not a date.*

Javier laid his fork atop his plate and gazed

across the table at her. When he spoke, his voice was low, coaxing. "Tell me something surprising about yourself."

Oh, crap.

It was a date.

"Tell me something surprising about yourself" was Javier's standard opening gambit every time he met an interested woman. Which was all of them. If they stared at him blankly or leaned forward to flash cleavage with a confession like "I'm not a real blonde," they didn't get a second chance. Javier didn't do stupid, and he didn't do boring.

He also didn't do guardian angels, but she had to say *something*. Something other than, "I have invisible wings and I watched you learn how to ride a tricycle when you were two." Or, "I was born in a realm called Nether-Netherland, where horses can fly and jackalopes work for the government."

She settled on, "I travel a lot for work."

Not the most exciting revelation, but it was the only thing she could say without lying. This was the first and last time they were ever going to meet like this. Face-to-face. Voice to voice. There was already so much subterfuge between them, she really wanted him to know something true. To exist in his memory as Sarah-the-person, not Sarah-the-mirage.

Javier leaned forward. "Me, too. Where have you traveled?"

"Everywhere," she answered simply. Everywhere *he'd* traveled, certainly. Thanks to him, she was familiar with every frequent-flier lounge on six continents. But she'd traveled much farther and far longer than that. Since before he was born. To worlds he'd never dreamed existed.

He arched a brow. Quizzed her on a few of his favorite places. Tried to trip her up on the differences between Kuala Lumpur and Jakarta. Was impressed that her knowledge of Russian teas rivaled his own. She'd had to fudge a few answers on purpose, just so he wouldn't think she was pulling her responses directly from his brain.

Ah, if only she *could* see into his brain. It would make this "date"—and her job—so much easier. Instead, she was forced to learn about him solely by observation. She couldn't interact, ask questions, or get feedback. Sarah never knew what he was thinking. Hell, she only knew for sure what he was planning if she happened to be looking over his shoulder when he signed a merger or scheduled a flight. And she couldn't watch him 24/7. Angels might not sleep, but guardians did have a monthly date with the Governing Council of Heavenly Beings to be debriefed on current assignments.

With a man like Javier, those hours apart from him were the most harrowing of her life. While she was busy assuring the Council that absolutely, the human was perfectly fine and perfectly safe and perfectly right on target for an inoperable coronary at age seventy, Javier would spontaneously decide to fly to Afghanistan or Somalia and vaccinate orphan children in the middle of a jungle in the path of an elephant stampede.

Sarah was an angel, not a homing pigeon, so as soon as she finished assuring the Council of her charge's continued safety, she'd have to frantically race to find him before he contracted malaria or got eaten by a tiger or fell into a snake pit.

Guarding him would go more smoothly once she made a graceful exit from his visible life. He was far easier to keep track of when she had wings and invisibility on her side.

"Well," she said brightly. "It was nice meeting you, but I've got to get going."

A glint came into his eye. A glint that one of his rivals had once referred to as "calculated skepticism." A glint that tore down façades faster than his competitors' legal teams could build them up. A glint that turned her belly into molten lava.

His smile was danger personified. "Are you staying here in Santita?"

"No," she said quickly. *He* was staying in Santita and she definitely didn't need him scouring the town for her.

"Do you have a car?"

She shook her head. She might be able to conjure up a car, but she'd never driven one.

First thing she'd probably do was drive it into a tree. "I'm taking the bus."

"Where are you heading?"

"To... Sucre?"

Damn. She hadn't thought up a backstory. She'd never *needed* a backstory. She'd never spoken to a human before, much less been boxed into a corner where she was forced to lie to one.

"No, you're not." He idly twirled the stem of his empty wineglass. "You don't have a hotel and you don't have a plan and you're definitely not going to Sucre. There are no buses until tomorrow. And nothing will convince me you were planning on walking two hundred kilometers in those shoes."

"I..."

"You're stuck here for the night, no matter what your plans might've been. Tomorrow morning, I've got a date with the local kids, but in the afternoon, I'll help you get to the right stop. The Sucre bus isn't until one o'clock anyway. We'll have plenty of time."

Sarah shook her head, frantic. "No, no, no. You really don't have to—"

"Of course I do. A woman traveling alone should not be hitching rides with strangers in the middle of nowhere. I'll go with you, and make sure they let you on a direct bus. It'll be safest."

Chivalry. Yay.

She stared at her pristine dinner plate in

dawning horror. If it was proving difficult to surreptitiously disappear in front of one person, it would be damn near impossible to do it in front of a busload of Bolivians. Not to mention, she couldn't trust that Javier wouldn't rappel down a landslide to rescue orphaned sloths before she had a chance to get out of the bus and fly back to find him. Her wings drooped in defeat.

No choice.

She was going to have to stay.

CHAPTER 3

Now that his growling stomach no longer dominated his thoughts, Javier viewed Sarah Phimm in a different light.

Candlelight, to be exact.

The sun had finally set, leaving a single yellow-orange flame to cast its warm glow on Sarah's cheeks, to lend extra shine to her golden ringlets, to sparkle softly on her... empty plate. Javier frowned. What if she hadn't already eaten? What if she didn't have any money and was simply too proud to accept his? What if she'd claimed to be staying "around" because she had nowhere else to go?

"*Do* you have a hotel?" he demanded suddenly.

Her eyes widened and she just as quickly glanced away. "I..."

She didn't. Great. "Do you have money? Tell me you have money."

"Uh..."

"Eat. I told you it was on me." He motioned to Doña Camila. "She needs to eat," he told her in the same tone he used to enforce hostile takeovers. He turned back to Sarah. "And then you'll come home with me."

"No-no-no-no," she stammered, her head shaking frantically. "I couldn't possibly—"

"You can have the guest bedroom and I'll sleep on the sofa in the main room. And I'm buying you breakfast *and* lunch before I put you on a bus going anywhere. And then—"

Her eyelashes did the weird fluttery thing as she mumbled something that sounded suspiciously like "extenuating circumstances" beneath her breath. Before he could ask her to speak up, Doña Camila was right there, patting her on the shoulder.

"She stays here," she informed Javier in a no-nonsense voice even a seasoned corporate raider wouldn't argue with. "There's no grandchildren tonight. You'll see her tomorrow."

Alrighty. Javier didn't understand the bit about grandchildren, but he supposed if Sarah had rented a room with Doña Camila, that explained how she knew the restaurant would be uncharacteristically open on a Sunday evening.

"Fine," he said, matching the sternness in Doña Camila's tone with an even steelier one of his own. "But see that she eats. On me." He handed her enough cash to feed an entire *fútbol* team and then rose to his feet before either woman could argue. "I'll be back tomorrow as soon as I finish with the kids."

He headed straight to the dentist's house where he fell asleep in his clothes on top of the still-made bed.

When the roosters heralded an early dawn, Javier forced his stiff muscles out of bed and into the shower, where the lack of hot water shocked the last wisps of sleep from his head.

He dressed quickly, pausing only to greet his hosts and scoop up the heavy sacks before heading out the door. He hoped to make it to the one-room schoolhouse before class began. It would be the best chance to speak to all the local children in the same place at the same time. Javier wanted the gift-giving to go as smoothly as possible. Particularly since he'd lost a big chunk of his supplies along the way.

The kids abandoned their makeshift soccer game the moment they saw him coming. Leaving the scarred, half-inflated ball to limp across the grass alone, they ran toward him like a herd of puppies.

Smiling at their innocent delight, he let them tear into the bags and divvy up the treasure as they pleased.

One of the first things that had struck him after spending time in less-privileged areas was the complete lack of a "Mine!" culture. He didn't know the families and the personalities and the town as well as these kids did, and he didn't have to. They were already dividing the clothes by size and need, art supplies by age and talent, toys by appropriateness and number of siblings.

Each child selected precisely one new thing to call their own before throwing themselves wholeheartedly into the pleasure of who they would surprise with the rest. This blanket for that baby sister, this hair clip for that pregnant mother, this hammer for that hardworking father, this book for that grandmother whose legs couldn't carry her into town anymore.

Despite not being able to provide all the items he'd started out with, Javier was more than certain that tonight, every inhabitant of this small town would have an unexpected gift. If that didn't make it a good Christmas, he didn't know what did.

No.

Not true.

Javier knelt to collect his now-empty sacks, and remained on his knees in the spiky grass. How many lives had corporations like his ruined? How many homes had been destroyed? Forests leveled? Rivers polluted? No amount of coloring books and clean socks could make up for something like that. People had *died* because of "industry leaders" like him. Because of mergers made, because of corners companies had cut. All in the name of the almighty dollar. The relentless bottom line. The ability to declare rising dividends for stockholders at a corporate gala and be greeted with standing ovations and raised glasses of champagne.

Javier was done turning a blind eye to the poor, the desperate, the helpless. But even if he spent the next thirty-five years atoning for the first thirty-five—which he fully intended to do—it was impossible for any one man to right a multibillion-dollar empire of wrongs.

And yet there was nothing to do but keep trying.

He flopped the empty burlap over his shoulder and pushed to his feet. Empty sacks didn't mean it was time to rest. Empty sacks meant it was time to refill the well. There were a thousand worthy towns like this one. Tens of thousands. If he lived to be eighty and it took one week to find a town in need and the rest of the month to deliver appropriate supplies, that ought to give him... five hundred and forty microscopic blips of goodness.

After a decade of destroying twice as much in a single day.

"*Señor*! Wait!"

Javier turned back toward the school. The children were seated quietly, pencils at the ready, as their schoolteacher jogged across the grass toward him.

"Thank you," she said, her smile beatific. "You are a godsend. I never doubted you would be back. Nor did the children."

Javier returned her smile, but his soul was hollow. He didn't deserve her thanks or her smile or her trust. He certainly didn't deserve the blind faith of innocent children. He didn't deserve anything but penance.

A gruff, "My pleasure," was all he said in reply. He wouldn't be seeing her, or the children, or this village again. It didn't do to get attached. Not when the only thing that kept him sane was moving on, and helping others to move forward.

"What are you doing for *noche buena?*" she asked with a warm smile.

As if he might have Christmas plans. Or loved ones to share them with.

"Do you know of any other towns that could use some holiday cheer?" he asked, well aware he hadn't answered her question. He'd learned the prize skills of avoidance and redirection at his father's knee.

"Towns?" the schoolteacher repeated doubtfully. "Yes, although I wouldn't call the place I have in mind a 'town.'"

Javier's blood flowed a little faster. "Who? Where?"

"South of here, far from the main roads but not too far from the Pilcomayo River, is a village desperately in need of help. Last year, the rainy season swept away most of their roads and many of their roofs. They are too poor to make the repairs and the government cannot help everyone. There is probably nothing you can do, but..."

But it was almost Christmas. And the rainy season was upon them again. If he didn't get the roofs fixed soon, those village kids would be dying of pneumonia before New Year's. He'd have to assess the damage, get supplies from anywhere he could... A thrill raced through him, just like it did whenever he'd confronted a corporation who declared hell would freeze over before they'd allow him to buy them out. Javier loved a challenge. And he always won.

This time, his smile was genuine. "If I leave now, can I make it by nightfall?"

All he had to do was get Miss Phimm squared away, and—

A long-suffering sigh sounded from right behind him. "I'm coming with you."

He whirled around.

Sarah Phimm. In a Carlos Santana T-shirt. And a traditional Bolivian peasant skirt. And steel-toed Doc Martens.

At least she'd left off the cupcake.

"You're coming where?"

"Wherever you're going." Her smile was angelic... and highly suspicious. She beamed at the schoolteacher. "I want to help, too."

He folded his arms over his chest. "What about the bus?"

"I don't prefer buses."

"Well, where I'm going requires a bus. How else would we get all the way to the Pilcomayo? On roller skates?"

"Four-wheel drive." She held up a tiny black fob and pressed a button. What looked like a sparkling new Toyota Land Cruiser gave a merry chirp in response.

Javier stared. Had he thought her stranded and penniless? She'd apparently out-poker-faced the world poker face champion. He couldn't help but be impressed.

"I'll take the ride," he said without hesitation. Even though it would have to be one-way.

Right now, Sarah might be thinking it would be a lark to visit a village in the middle of nowhere. But she couldn't begin to guess how much work a project like this would be, or how much time it could take. He'd be spending Christmas Eve—*noche buena*—beneath a lean-to in the middle of nowhere. As eccentric as she was, Sarah undoubtedly had somewhere better to be. People who loved her. Who missed her. Expected her home.

He smiled to hide the dark turn his mind had taken. "I'll chip in for gas if you let me drive."

"You'll pay for everything and like it." She tossed him the keys.

He caught them with one hand and turned back to the schoolteacher. "I'll be on the road within the hour."

"Wonderful. With four-wheel drive, you can definitely make it before nightfall." She smiled and handed him a scrap of paper. She'd sketched a map on one side and written a name on the other. "Ask for Alvaro. Tell him you are a friend of mine. He will give you shelter. And... thank you."

"Thank *you*." Javier tucked the paper into his wallet. She would never know just how badly he needed this. He kissed her cheek, waved to the children, and cut over to the SUV. Sarah was already in the passenger seat.

He hauled open the door and swung himself inside. The driver's seat was roomy, comfy, clean. Everything about the car sparkled like new. Power mirrors and lumbar seats, heated steering wheel, GPS-enabled smart screen with rearview cameras... Where had she rented this thing? A factory showroom? How had it even gone a yard down the road without attracting a healthy coating of mud and dust? He turned the key in the ignition, half expecting to see a row of zeroes across the odometer.

Nope. It read "1952." He smiled wryly. The year of his mother's birth. There was an old family photo from that year, back home on Javier's desk. Framed. His mom as a chipmunk-cheeked infant, bundled in his grandmother's arms. He'd never gotten to meet his grandmother, but he always imagined her looking exactly as she did in that photo, with her dark hair in soup-can curls, her baby in her arms, and her skirt awhirl as if—

Javier cut a sharp glance at Sarah.

Her skirt was identical to the traditional Bolivian garb his grandmother had worn in the photo.

He shook his head and settled his hand on the gear stick. He was being fanciful, which wasn't like him in the least. Of course Sarah's skirt looked like his grandmother's. All Bolivian traditional skirts were similar. That was the point of tradition. It stayed the same. He didn't even know if her skirt was of the same colors. All he had was a black-and-white photograph that had gone yellow and brittle before he'd even been born.

As for the 1952 glowing up at him from the dash? Nothing otherworldly there, either. All cars had to pass that number and every other potentially meaningful number, as their odometer clocked the miles. Or kilometers, as the case may be.

He needed to get his head out of the past and focus on the future. Pick up his luggage from the dentist's house and hit the road. "Plenty of time" was never as much time as you thought, and anything could happen on the road between here and there. He glanced into the second row of seats to see if Sarah had thought ahead to bring her luggage.

She had. One small carry-on bag.

His was right beside it.

"You brought my *luggage?*" he blurted in surprise.

Her eyes closed. Not the weird fluttery thing she sometimes did, but a comparatively normal I'm-in-so-much-trouble squeezing of the eyes.

"I took a few liberties," she mumbled.

He thought about that. Clearly she expected some sort of retribution. But why? It was just a suitcase. She hadn't stolen it from him—she'd brought it to him. Thanks to her foresight, they'd be on the road that much faster. Matter of fact, if it weren't for her, he might not be on the road at all.

So he said, "Thanks," and slid the gearshift into first. As soon as they were on the highway, he messed with the radio until he found a genre he liked. The farther they got from Padilla, the weaker the signal would become, but for now they would have music.

As if he'd conjured it up through wishful thinking, the opening of Santana's *They All Went to Mexico* drifted from the speakers.

"Know this one?" he asked innocently. Nobody knew this one. It had never charted.

Sarah snorted and shot him a look of such comical disbelief, he could barely contain his laughter. "Word for word, trust me."

He shook his head, grinning. "I don't trust. You'll have to prove yourself."

He cranked up the radio, letting the opening riffs engulf them like a tidal wave. Now what would she do? Either she'd gotten her shirt at a thrift shop, or she would at least know the chorus. Bonus points if she—

Sarah's voice blended perfectly with the radio from the very first syllable.

Javier couldn't hide his surprise. Sure, this obscure 1983 crossover with Willie Nelson was a certain demographic had *heard* of, and perhaps roller-skated to. But it was no "Hotel California." Only someone who *liked* this song would memorize the lyrics.

Someone like him.

Hands on the wheel and eyes facing forward, he opened his mouth and sang along with her. He expected his off-key caterwaul to immediately ruin the moment. There was a reason he only sang in the shower and the car, when no one was around to overhear.

But Sarah didn't even pause. If she noticed anything unmelodic about his voice, she gave no outward sign. Instead, she leaned forward and turned the dash into an impromptu drum kit, pounding along with the rhythm and ending the set by twirling an imaginary drumstick and flinging it in his direction.

He caught it and flung it right back. She pretended to catch it in her teeth and spit it on the floor between them. He cracked up. The music was too loud to even discern the sound of his laughter. It took him an extra beat to realize that he and pretty, kooky Sarah Phimm were drumming beats and clowning to hair metal as if they'd known each other all their lives.

She'd made him laugh. Actually *laugh*. For the first time since... the hearing.

Javier swallowed. Had it really been that long since he'd laughed? He'd assumed he'd lost all his friends because they'd never really been his friends to begin with. But maybe they weren't the only ones who had changed.

He'd been fun once, hadn't he? When was the last time he'd played air guitar or felt completely unselfconscious in front of another person?

Probably not since high school.

He gripped the wheel a little tighter. Yeah, high school. Sophomore year. Sadie Hawkins dance with a stoner girl who wore shoes just like Sarah's. He'd gone as her date because she'd been brave enough to ask him, and ended up having the most fun he'd had at any school dance, ever. Despite not knowing any of the same moves. As awkward as they were together, she hadn't seen any reason not to flounder front and center, right in front of the speakers. They'd owned that dance floor.

The next week, he'd turned sixteen and started apprenticing for his father. No more sports, no more dances. No more patchouli-scented girls in reinforced boots. From that birthday on, everything was about making money. Pleasing his father. Starting his own company. Keeping his eye on the bottom line.

Yeah. That'd all turned out great. He'd given up on all of it. And he shouldn't feel too cozy toward Sarah, either. She was much cooler than anticipated, but even the coolest of chicks had to walk away sometime. And she wouldn't be back. Neither would he. He'd be... wherever he was needed. He passed through Malibu only a handful of days in the year. The rest of the time, even *he* didn't know where he'd be from day to day, week to week.

It was a good thing his father had conditioned him not to count on anyone except himself. Otherwise this dull ache inside his chest might be misinterpreted as loneliness.

He grimaced. *Los Rodriguez* didn't get lonely. They didn't need other people. As his father was fond of telling a much younger Javier, "Right now, you need me, but I don't need you. And someday, you won't need me either." It was a mark of pride. A goal to work toward. The mythical, fantastical state of not needing anyone. Of not caring about anything but success.

By the time his father passed, Javier had learned the lesson far too well.

Was it too late to unlearn it? He glanced over at Sarah. Her face was turned toward the window and he couldn't see her expression. Maybe she was trying to sleep. He turned the radio down.

Her face swiveled to his, a question in her eyes.

Well, he had her attention. What was the plan now?

"Uh..." His mind went blank. Javier whipped his gaze back to the road and heroically withstood the impulse to face-palm. Dozens of girlfriends, one hundred international takeovers and a billion dollars later, and he'd still somehow managed to revert to the eloquence level of his fifteen-year-old self?

No. He was still Javier Rodriguez, pillar of confidence, nerves of steel.

So why did spending time with Sarah feel so different?

"You wore a Lakers jersey yesterday," he found himself saying. As far as exposing his deep insights and razor-sharp wit went, it wasn't much. But maybe it would at least get them talking again.

"Mm," she answered noncommittally.

True, it hadn't exactly been a question. And while she'd turned out to actually know the lyrics for the artist's music featured on her concert tee, the presence of sports paraphernalia often said less about a person's athletic fanaticism and more about that person's geography. Are you from Chicago? Then you've got a Bears hat somewhere in your closet. Malibu? Sure, maybe the Lakers. Although a jersey still seemed a little more meaningful than a ball cap.

"You like basketball?" he tried again.

Her eyes widened as if she'd never considered the possibility before in her life.

"I'm familiar with it," she answered hesitantly, as if it might've been a trick question.

And, honestly. Wasn't it? Hadn't part of him been waiting for her to say she did, just so he could test her with pedantic trivia to prove she wasn't a real fan? Classy. But now that he'd called himself out on his dickishness, he might as well carry it through.

"Do you have a jersey because you actually *like* the Lakers, or do you have a Lakers jersey just because they're from California?"

She wrinkled her nose at him as if he'd lost his mind. "They're not 'from California,'" she said in disbelief, as if he'd suggested Santa Claus lived in the tropics. "The Lakers were the old Detroit Gems, relocated to Minneapolis. They picked their new name in honor of Minnesota's ten thousand lakes. The team didn't move to LA until 1960."

He stared at her. Speechless. Words utterly and completely failed him.

"They're not 'from California,'" she repeated stubbornly and lifted her chin in the air.

"Marry me."

"What?" She reared back in nothing short of full-on horror.

He shrugged winningly. "I always said I'd marry the first girl who gave me that answer."

"You've never said that in your entire life!"

"Well, I thought it plenty of times. Is that a no?"

"It's a 'you're crazy,'" she stammered.

He gave a slow smile. "Crazy in a good way?"

"Crazy like Elgin Baylor scoring sixty-one points in a playoff game and keeping the record for fifty years."

"So, crazy-awesome then. I'll take it."

"You oughtta take your meds," she muttered under her breath.

Once again, Javier had to grip the wheel to stop himself from laughing. He'd twice made *People* magazine's list of "50 Most Eligible Bachelors" and he'd just gotten shot down by a Santana fan in a peasant skirt.

He slid another look her way. She was something else.

With or without a plastic cupcake on her head, Sarah was undeniably pretty. Naturally lovely, not a cosmetically altered Barbie clone. Eccentric, sure, but with a big heart. Why else would she give a guy a ride to the middle of nowhere in her factory-condition SUV?

She was refreshingly... *real.* He'd spent his adult life knowing everyone in his private world feared him, and then the past few years knowing the entire world would be better off hating him. He hadn't been able to be "just Javier" in... well, in a long time.

If ever.

And yet here, with her, he was singing off-key and playing air drums and poking fun at himself and having one of the best afternoons in years.

Crap. Afternoon. Already the sunlight was growing dim. He glanced down at the odometer. They were almost to the river. Playtime was over. As soon as she saw the village—or lack thereof—Sarah would be on her way. Anybody would. He couldn't blame her. He was still humbled she'd allowed him to take up this much of her time.

The most important lesson he'd ever learned was not to get attached.

CHAPTER 4

Sarah stopped drumming a microsecond before the SUV tires skidded to a stop. Not that they'd been clipping along at a speedy pace to begin with. They couldn't.

Over the past several kilometers, the pothole-sprinkled paved road had given way to a gravel road, which had given way to a dirt road, which had given way to a mud path, which had led them to what had possibly once been a fairly serviceable bridge.

For, like, horses. Or foot traffic. Maybe.

It was barely wider than the SUV. The sides might have concrete supports under the layers of caked-on dirt and mud, but the bottom consisted solely of wooden slats. Moldered slats. Broken slats. Sections of no slats at all, where, forty feet below, wicked currents churned over layers of jagged rock.

Javier put the SUV back into gear.

"What are you doing?" Sarah squeaked.

But she already knew. This? This was why Javier Rodriguez needed a keeper. When he had a goal, every ounce of his concentration, every cell in his body, laser-focused on achieving that goal. He never knew defeat because he never acknowledged opposition, much less setbacks. And he certainly wasn't going to let a mere death trap stand in the way of him and some no-name village in the middle of nowhere.

"I'm driving across," Javier answered reasonably, as if anyone in their right mind would've come to the same decision. "We can't abandon your car. The village is on the other side of this river. Driving across makes the most sense."

"Absolutely not," Sarah said flatly.

His eyebrows rose as if he were honestly shocked that in her world, respect for one's life outweighed foolhardy hero-complex risks.

"What's your—Oh." His eyebrows lowered and he nodded in belated understanding. "*Your* car. Right." He shifted back into neutral and set the parking brake. "Thanks so much for taking me this far. I really appreciate it. Let me give you some money to cover the detailing and probably a new pair of shocks..."

Sarah tilted her face heavenward but the only illumination was the dome light. She didn't care about the *car*. She cared about his freaking *life*. Why was her job so hard?

He'd finally given her the opening she'd been looking for, in terms of disappearing without suspicion, and she couldn't even take it. Firstly because she'd never driven anything. Sure, she'd been right next to him during Drivers' Ed and pretty much every second of rush hour traffic since. But she'd witnessed enough first-time driver mishaps to know there was no chance of her pulling off a successful three-point turn... on sloped mud... in an unfamiliar stick-shift behemoth... and navigating out of sight without raising suspicion or totaling the stupid thing worse than the bridge was likely to do.

And the bridge! As long as she stayed glued to his side, she could ensure the bridge would last another day. If she drove off, she wouldn't be there to save him from rapids or pit vipers or food poisoning. Javier could find trouble in seconds. Even if she managed to drive away semi-competently and ditch the car around the first curve, that was more than enough time for a man who thought *this* was a good idea to get into a lot more trouble.

"Drive."

His fingers froze on his open wallet. "What?"

"Drive," she repeated, gesturing toward the dilapidated bridge in defeat. "But I'm going on record as saying this is a terrible idea, and you have to stop risking your life on the off chance you might be able to help others."

"Why should I?" His bafflement was genuine, damn him. "My life doesn't have any more value than anyone else's. Have you checked Twitter lately? Some would say my life doesn't have any value at all. But here I am. I might as well do what I can to make a difference, don't you think?"

Sarah glared at him in silence. *I'll get fired if you die* seemed the wrong response here, as was *I've been half in love with you for years, so... yeah. Your life matters more to me than a whole village of strangers.* They were going to have to agree to disagree.

"Are you driving or not?"

"I'm driving." He lowered the parking brake and shifted into gear.

The SUV inched across the bridge. Tires slipped, planks groaned and cracked, but Sarah kept it from falling apart.

When they reached the other side, Javier grinned at her as if he'd never had a doubt in the world. But he shot an unnerved glance toward the rearview mirror. "Where's the department of transportation when you need them? They really ought to fix that bridge."

Sarah crossed her arms and stared straight ahead. He was right. "They" should. But they wouldn't, because there *was* no "they." The Bolivian government could barely handle what was already on their plate. Which left who? Sarah was contractually prohibited from performing any miracles that removed her focus from her assigned client. And as to other guardian angels in the vicinity? As far as she knew, there weren't any. The solitary life of a guardian angel wasn't exactly the most-requested track at Uni.

Javier coaxed the SUV along the increasingly indiscernible path. "Don't worry so much. I knew the bridge had to be stronger than it looked." He grinned. "And maybe I'm just lucky."

She gaped at him as if he'd lost his mind. Maybe he had. That bridge was held together by spit and sunshine. If she hadn't helped it along, he'd be trapped between a twisted SUV and jagged rocks right now. *She* was his luck, both good and bad. And she definitely couldn't trust him to be alone for a second.

He killed the engine when they finally rolled up on the village.

A dozen flimsy, weather-beaten shacks. Rusty tin roofs missing whole sections. A few crops, a few chickens, two cows. That was it. No cars. No stores. Not even a church.

"Perfect." Javier's eyes shone.

Sarah sighed. She knew where this was going.

"This is where I'm meant to be," he continued happily. "These are *precisely* the people who could use some Christmas spirit."

"And some roofs," she muttered.

"Definitely new roofs. And a school! Can you believe there's no school?"

"Gobsmacked."

"Come on, let's go find Alvaro."

"Yay." She slid out of her seat, vaporizing every mosquito within a three-yard radius of the car. He was *not* getting yellow fever before they even grabbed their luggage. If she caught it fast enough, she could zap viruses and germs right out of his bloodstream, but prevention was the best cure.

A handful of cute, barefoot children in ill-fitting clothes bounded up to them, bubbling with rapid-fire Spanish. "Who are you? What are you doing here?"

Javier crouched down to eye level. "We're looking for a man named Alvaro. Do any of you know Alvaro?"

"Grandfather!" two of the children screamed in unison.

A man whose body seemed twice as old as his face limped over to them. *"Buenas tardes."*

"Good afternoon, sir. I was told to ask for you when I arrived." Javier showed him the paper the schoolteacher had drawn.

The man's eyes softened. "You're friends with my daughter? Come. Eat with us. You must spend the night."

Chicken and rice was straightforward enough, but it was immediately apparent that spending the night would be more problematic. Alvaro's tiny house could barely offer standing room to its inhabitants. The thin walls shook as thunder rent the air.

Cold rain fell like automatic gunfire against the metal roof, slithering through the cracks and drizzling the two-room interior with a miserable layer of wet. A puddle grew in the middle of the living area. The children curled up around the edges, careful to stay between the growing puddle and the slick slime of the damp walls.

Javier lowered his mouth to Sarah's ear. "Do you have a tent, by any chance?"

Sarah nodded quickly, closing her eyes as she adjusted the contents of the trunk. If Javier needed a tent, he'd get the most miraculous tent she could muster.

"Sweet." Javier turned to Alvaro and his wife. "I'm here to fix the roofs in this village. I don't yet have the supplies, but we do have an extra tent that will keep the children safe and dry until I can do more."

Sarah hesitated. If the tent was for this family and not for Javier personally, she wasn't supposed to share the miracle love. If she followed the letter of her contract, she probably ought to unmiracle the tent and claim she'd forgotten to bring it after all. But it was already in the SUV... And these kids... And that roof...

It wasn't worth getting fired over and not be able to guard *anyone* anymore, but if she justified the gray area by claiming a tent for the family would directly affect her assigned subject's peace of mind—and then was very careful not to stretch any more rules—she might get through her end-of-month review with her title still intact.

Decision made, Sarah led Javier to the trunk and watched his eyes sparkle when he saw the size of the tent.

"This baby will fit everyone! It's perfect!" In

his delight, he gave her a quick, excited hug he probably wouldn't even remember doing, and launched himself into the task of setting the tent up alongside the shack before the freezing drizzle coalesced into an outright downpour.

Sarah, on the other hand, was perfectly motionless. She couldn't move. She couldn't breathe. She could barely even think.

Javier had *touched* her. Happily. Voluntarily. *Consciously*.

He might've accidentally trod upon one of her feathers a time or two without knowing any different, but this—this! Her heart pounded.

She'd never even dreamed about being hugged. Not by him, not by anybody. Sure, people hugged each other as much in heaven as they did on Earth or among the bureaucracies of Nether-Netherland. But the life of a nonmanagerial guardian angel was a life of unending solitude. Constantly surrounded by throngs of people, including the one you cared the most about in the whole world, but doomed to remain unnoticed and invisible for eternity. No one to talk to, to laugh with, to cry with, to love. Endless loneliness.

Until now.

She'd been *hugged*. By *Javier!*

Sarah rubbed her arms and shivered. It had been over in an instant, but she would remember it forever.

Javier saw her shiver just as he drove the final stake. He was instantly at her side. "You're cold. Of course you're cold. Why are you standing outside? Here, get in the car. I'm going to put the other tent up far enough away to give them a little privacy. My tent isn't as big as this one, but soon you'll be warm. Or at least dry."

She nodded, and let him tuck her back into the passenger seat.

As soon as she was safe from the elements, he dashed to Alvaro's leaky house to usher the occupants into their new shelter. Her miracles might not be supposed to affect other people, but the children's smiles and the look of utter gratitude in Alvaro's eyes warmed her to her soul.

Once the family was settled, Javier unhooked a small, two-person tent from the bottom of his backpack and had it staked and functional within seconds. He tossed her bag inside after his, and then motioned for her to join him. In a daze, she did.

How many nights had she passed with him in this very tent? Careful to stay out of reach, yet close enough to watch over him as he slept? This time, it would be different.

This time would be very, *very* different.

He unrolled a thin mat and wadded up a pair of clean towels to use as pillows. The look he shot her was nothing short of sheepish. "It's not a penthouse suite, but..."

"It's lovely." She lay down beside him and stretched out her limbs as naturally as she could, which was undoubtedly as awkwardly and self-consciously as possible.

She was lying. On a mat. With Javier Rodriguez.

Her foot twitched. Then her arm twitched. Then her eye twitched. Her wings were tucked beneath her as tightly as possible but she could swear that even her feathers twitched. Every single inch of her body was completely on edge. Horribly, deliciously, hyperaware of the very strong, very male, very *right-there-oh-my-God* sexy human lying next to her in the tent.

Every other woman who'd ever lain next to him had been a million times more jaded and experienced than Sarah ever would be. Much like driving a stick shift across a collapsing bridge in the middle of Bolivia, watching someone do something and doing it yourself were two totally different things. Not that there was any chance of romance. Which was lucky, since she'd never be able to live up to even the worst of his memories.

In fact, Sarah couldn't even think of a time Javier had spent the night with a woman he wasn't romantically involved with. Making this completely new territory. For both of them. Unless he was thinking sharing a tent meant sharing their bodies... Her heartbeat reached supersonic speeds. She couldn't take the pressure. The anticipation. The panic.

She hoped he wouldn't try anything.

Oh, God, she hoped he *would*.

She tilted her head, millimeter by millimeter, until she could see his face out of the corner of her eye.

His eyes were closed. His lips, slightly parted. His breath, even. He was beautiful. He was... sleeping. Sleeping!

Sarah swallowed hard and did her best not to reach out and touch his face. It was her duty to watch over him, not to let him in her heart. Or her arms.

It was going to be a very long night.

CHAPTER 5

The next morning, Sarah made a huge production out of stretching and yawning and "waking up." Playing pretend was way better than the alternative, which would be admitting she'd gotten an eyeful of morning wood as Javier crawled over her to unzip the tent.

Face flaming, she waited until he was gone before conjuring up a fresh set of clothes.

And then immediately unconjured them.

Damn.

Passing as human meant she couldn't just *be* clean and groomed and dressed. She'd have to drag her bag into Alvaro's bathroom and stand under the makeshift shower for ten minutes, or at least until her hair got wet. She sighed.

Being "human" was even lousier than she'd thought. Not that Javier showed any signs of flagging.

After a breakfast of fresh coffee and hand-made tortillas cooked over an open flame, he was ready to conquer the day. Sarah hadn't been able to avoid breakfast altogether, but had managed to only take a few sips of her heavily-sugared coffee. Partly because she had no idea how her angel stomach would react to human comestibles. But mostly because, *coffee,* bleh, gross. It smelled *so* much better than it tasted.

As soon as they'd washed their cups, they were back on the road, heading toward the last hardware store they remembered passing, some twenty kilometers away. Which meant crossing the death bridge again.

Javier seemed to have regained full trust in the bridge's structural integrity. Not for the first time, Sarah wished she could make his confidence a reality. But rules were rules, and the last thing she wanted to do was lose her position and not be there to protect him.

While they gassed up the SUV, Javier made friends with the service station attendants. During a spending frenzy at the hardware store, he made friends with the entire family who owned it. When they ducked into the grocery store to load up on more supplies, he charmed the cashiers and the stock boy and even the mother of three in front of them in line.

Javier believed he'd become a wildly successful business mogul due to the influence of his asshole father, but Sarah knew better. Javier became wildly successful because Javier was *Javier*. His sincerity shone in his face. His smile sparkled in his eyes. His unfailing eagerness and well-deserved confidence infused every word, every tone, every gesture.

If Javier said the villagers would be safe and dry by Christmas, then by God, the villagers would be safe and dry by Christmas. He'd follow through or die trying.

He'd already sweet-talked the school around the corner into agreeing to take on the village kids. It was too far to walk, of course, but if Javier could come up with transportation, they could find desks for everyone.

Within seconds, he was on his cellphone, ordering up a bus.

The mechanic across the street agreed to loan his trailer to the cause. Javier insisted on renting, not borrowing, which would surprise no one who knew him. Least of all Sarah. He'd had a complex about not causing a burden or expense ever since the government had put his life into stark perspective.

He affixed the trailer to the SUV's towing hitch and started loading up. In less than an hour, the once nondescript vehicle more closely resembled the Grinch's overflowing sleigh as he pulled away from Whoville with stolen Christmas cheer.

Maybe she should tie an antler to her head to fit in.

Javier's mood stayed jaunty and buoyant until the headlights beamed onto the one detail he'd forgotten during his Bob-Vila-of-the-jungle shopping spree.

The bridge.

The SUV had made it across twice with no problem, but now it was stacked to the ceiling and they were towing another umpteen pounds. Much trickier.

Sarah hadn't forgotten. Sarah was busy wishing her miracles included the ability to usurp free will, so that she could erase this and all other harebrained hero-complex schemes from Javier's thick skull once and for all.

"Maybe you should get out and walk across," he suggested in a low voice. "I'll follow with the trailer."

Like hell.

"My weight isn't going to make a difference to whether those slats can support a trillion-ton trailer," she pointed out.

This was a true statement. Not because of the physics—although she was pretty sure math would support her theory that *nothing* had any business crossing this bridge—but because she was going to miracle-up safe passage for both of them.

"But you have to promise me," she continued seriously. "If we make it across alive, you *will not* take that risk ever again, or allow anyone else to do so. You've already made friends with everyone in the province. They can haul individual parts across piecemeal if they have to. No more heavy trailers."

She was forbidden from directly interfering with human lives, but *God* had she needed to get that off her chest. She'd been dying to talk sense into the man since he first learned to talk. Now that she was corporeal, there was no way she was letting him do something this stupid without giving him a reality check.

Whether he listened or not was another story.

He nodded slowly. "Okay. I can live with that. You make a good point."

She let out a slow breath she hadn't realized she was holding. He'd listened, and he'd agreed. And she trusted him. The old Javier might've used words as a weapon to manipulate his opponents, but the new Javier—*this* Javier—took his word very seriously indeed.

"Good. Thank you."

They eased across the bridge.

Sarah kept them safe, but drove the point home with augmented volume on every creak and groan of rotted wood. Plenty of dislodged debris tumbled into the rocks below for effect.

She wasn't adding these things. She was merely done hiding them.

Javier was white-knuckled when they reached the other side. He checked the rearview mirror three times in a row, as if he couldn't quite believe the bridge was still standing.

Good. Maybe he would think twice from now on. Thinking twice was an excellent survival skill.

When they reached the village, all the able-bodied villagers—and several who didn't quite qualify, but were determined to help out anyway—met the SUV and immediately began helping unload the trailer.

Sarah was glad for the extra hands. She didn't want to seem unhelpful, but she also didn't want to leave Javier's side for even a second to go fetch this tool or measure those dimensions. He might not cross the bridge with a heavy trailer ever again, but there was plenty of other trouble he could get into the moment she turned her back.

That was how "accidents" happened. If an assigned human appeared at the Pearly Gates prior to their scheduled arrival, it was the fault of the guardian angel, not the unprotected mortal. Besides, no punishment would ever be as fierce as the prospect of unrelenting guilt for the rest of eternity. Sarah could never let that happen.

Her one and only goal was keeping Javier safe. By hook or by crook. Come hell or high water. No matter the cost. He would be the *picture* of health on his seventieth birthday, dammit. Well, except for the impending coronary.

She was not going to think about what would come after. Nope, she was definitely not going to think about how her chosen path doomed her to spend year after year keeping someone safe only to have them die anyway.

And then be assigned someone else, some other lovable baby who would grow into a strong, complex adult whose end days were already marked on her calendar.

Sometimes being a guardian angel sucked.

Maybe most of the time.

The sky darkened, and before long it began to drizzle. Everyone kept working. Sarah stood at the foot of a ladder, keeping it safe and steady as Javier climbed around Alvaro's roof like a spider monkey. She'd loved all her mortal assignments in their own way, but none had touched her heart the way Javier did. What he saw when he looked in the mirror and what she saw from up above were such totally different perspectives. He didn't think of himself as worthy or deserving. And yet he was one of the best men she'd ever had the privilege of knowing.

After centuries of watching over humans, that was saying a lot.

He poked his head over the edge of the roof and grinned down at her. She grinned back involuntarily. With a wink, he was gone again.

Okay, yes. Plus he was cute. He was certainly the first human she'd ever fantasized about kissing. But even then, she'd been well aware of the impossibility of interaction. She was a thousand-year-old virgin who had seen it all. And he'd never even known she existed.

Until now. She shivered. After decades of literally being invisible to him, it was very heady for her to actually be seen. She felt exposed... and yet not. He could see her, but he couldn't see *her*. He didn't know the real Sarah. And never would.

Not that that stopped her from wishing.

By dusk, three of the worst roofs were patched. All the fresh food and dry blankets had been distributed. Javier had been invited to dinner in so many houses, she was afraid the overabundance of rice would burst his stomach.

After they said their good-byes to the last of the happy families, he looped his fingers with hers as they walked back to their tent. He was talking a mile a minute about everything they'd done and everything they still had yet to do, and probably hadn't even noticed they were walking hand in hand.

Sarah, for her part, couldn't hear a single word he said. She didn't see him, didn't hear him, didn't smell him, didn't recognize any aspect of the environment around them, because her entire world had shrunk until all it included was the tactile sensation of her hand in his.

His hand was warm, his fingers strong and slightly calloused from wielding hammers. Her hand felt tiny and soft and... safe, wrapped up in his.

Safe. What a wonderful, ridiculous feeling for a guardian angel to have.

She was the one who kept others safe. She was the angel. She was immortal. She performed miracles. There was absolutely nothing a human could give her that she wasn't perfectly capable of providing for herself.

Except... *this*.

Companionship. Joy. A shared moment.

His footsteps slowed. She wasn't certain when he'd stopped talking, but he was silent now. He took her other hand in his. They were alone beneath the light of the stars, only a sliver of moon to catch the edge of his features and illuminate him staring down at her the same way she was staring up at him.

The rain had stopped, and the soft breeze rustling amongst the leaves sounded like the fluttering of a thousand angel wings.

He lifted her hands to his shoulders and she immediately twined them around his neck. He was so close. Larger than life. She wasn't sure whether he leaned down or she stretched up, but the distance closed between them until the only stars she could see were the ones reflected in his eyes.

His mouth brushed against hers. Gentle. Seeking permission.

Her lips parted. When his mouth brushed hers for a second time, she was ready. She held him as tight as she'd ever dreamed, as tight as she dared, and swept her tongue into his mouth to taste him.

Bliss. He was everything she'd ever imagined. More than she'd ever hoped for. His hands were in her hair, holding her to him as if afraid she might let go. As if she would *ever* let go. She clung to him, opening her mouth and her heart, recognizing this moment for the miracle it was. A taste of something that could never be hers.

She loved him, but she couldn't have him. Had never had him. He didn't truly know who he was kissing. And she couldn't tell him any more than she could keep him.

All she had was this moment. This man, beneath her fingertips. This heart, beating against hers. This breeze and this starlight, encircling them with magic.

This memory, to cherish forever.

CHAPTER 6

Javier went to bed with the worst case of blue balls he'd ever experienced in his life.

Knowing Sarah was right beside him, giving an equally Oscar-worthy performance of Faking Sleep, did not help matters. Just saying her name in his head made his heart beat faster.

He shouldn't have kissed her.

He hadn't *meant* to kiss her. He hadn't kissed anyone since becoming a professional nomad. He hadn't wanted to. He hadn't felt worthy of anyone's affection, and he certainly hadn't felt like he deserved to experience anything as elusive as happiness.

And then—Sarah.

Everything about her surprised him. Not just her bizarre outfits, although the acid-washed denim romper and hot pink jelly shoes were a sight to behold. He hadn't seen jelly shoes since 1985, when his sister had chucked a similar pair out her bedroom window, claiming her entire foot had scabbed over from chafing against inflexible plastic.

The thing about Sarah was that she seemed to actually understand him. To *believe* in him. Not in a sycophantic or lemming sort of way, either. She certainly wasn't shy about making her opinions known when she disagreed with his decisions or accused him of being headstrong.

That, too, was refreshing. He'd already gone from the mogul who could do no wrong to the villain who could do no right. Having someone view him objectively and still choose to support him was something he'd never anticipated experiencing again.

And how was it possible she'd be willing to spend Christmas repairing tin roofs in the Bolivian jungle? In the past, he'd never spent time with a woman without providing chauffeured transportation and luxury accommodations. And here he was, borrowing Sarah's five-star wheels and sharing a tent whose primary extravagance was mosquito netting. Not exactly living the fairy tale. His sole claim to chivalry was gallantly rolling up a towel for her to use as a pillow.

Suave. Real suave.

And yet kissing her had just seemed right. Holding her hand. Touching her cheek. Tasting her lips.

Not that there was any future in it, of course.

He'd sworn that he would never again put his happiness above anyone else's. His crusade to fix the world would consume every waking hour for the rest of his life. That's how it had to be. No one could be expected to willingly join him in such an undertaking. And falling for a woman would make her both a liability to and a distraction from his cause, neither of which he could afford.

But, man. He sure wished he was still kissing her.

No, not even that. At least, not necessarily that. He'd be happy just curling up beside her, one arm around her waist and the other going slowly numb, trapped beneath her shoulders. Snuggled tight. The pins and needles would be worth it, just to have held her in his arms.

He rubbed his face and groaned. At this rate, he was never going to fall asleep.

He gave in to one of his desires and rolled onto his side, facing her. He didn't sling an arm over her hips or touch her in any way—it wouldn't be fair to either of them to start something doomed to go nowhere—but at least, from this angle, he could smell her hair. She always smelled freshly-showered, no matter what they'd been doing. It wasn't a flowery scent or a citrusy scent or any other scent he could put into words. She just smelled like Sarah. Perfect.

He fell asleep smiling.

In his dream, he floated out of the tent. He was still with Sarah, but not on the hard ground in the mountains. They were somewhere soft, somewhere heavenly, suspended in a luxurious feather bed overlooking the sea.

He opened his eyes. It was morning. He was still on his side, still in the tent, still on the ground. Although he was awake, the odd sensation of reclining on a feather bed still remained.

Sarah was awake, too.

He smiled at her. She grimaced back at him. His smile widened. Maybe she wasn't a morning person. He used to think he wasn't, either, but his dad had forced him out of bed every morning at dawn until habit kicked in, and now to do otherwise would be unthinkable. Maybe she just needed some practice.

"You can get up first," he murmured. "I'll let you have first dibs on the bathroom."

"I can't," she said quietly. "You go ahead."

He grinned, a flash of stubbornness goading him to keep teasing her. "Oh no, I insist. Ladies first."

"I *can't*," she said through gritted teeth. She turned her face away, but it sounded almost as though she'd muttered something like, "You're on my wing."

He'd reflexively rolled away before his mind processed her words. "I'm on your what?"

"Nothing." She sprang to her feet far too energetically, even for a morning person. "I'm fine. You're fine. We're all fine."

He shook his head, certain he was right. "Did

you say I was on your *wing*? Why would you say I was on your wing?"

She glared at him, clearly exasperated, and then let out a low sigh. "Fine. I'll tell you. They'll wipe your memory anyway after the end-of-month debriefing. I'm your guardian angel and you were lying on one of my wings. I don't think we should sleep together anymore. And probably no more kissing."

"The who what?" he stammered, certain he'd misheard her after all. He bolted upright as the fog cleared. "I'm sorry, did you just claim to be an *angel*?"

Her shoulders slumped resignedly. "I don't know why I thought I could fool you for more than a few hours in the first place. It's too much work to be human. I'm tired of pretending to eat and sleep. And as cute as you are, it was no picnic having my wing pinned to the ground all night. I'm going to be sore for days."

Um, wow.

Javier stared at her wordlessly. To say he was suffering the first inkling of doubt as to her sanity would be putting it mildly. He was a logical man. Angels did not wear cupcake headbands and drive stick shifts. Therefore, his dream girl was having a psychotic break, or... okay, yeah. She was insane.

Of course, she was still hot and still otherwise awesome, so perhaps he shouldn't be too hasty.

"You're an angel," he repeated slowly. Questioningly.

She nodded. "A guardian angel. Your guardian angel."

"So... you do miracles?"

Her eyes narrowed as if she suspected a trap. "When necessary."

"Well, do one now."

"Do one what?"

"A miracle. Prove you have the power."

"I'm an angel, not your monkey. I don't have to prove anything. You're not even supposed to know I exist. I'll be lucky if I don't get fired for this. It's a very exclusive guild."

"I see." He tapped his chin. "How exactly does one become part of the angel guild?"

She crossed her arms over her chest and glared at him. Eventually, she muttered, "You're either born or chosen. Or the third way."

Huh? Was that supposed to make sense? He waited, but that seemed to be the extent of the explanation. "Well, that was enlightening."

"I'm not allowed to talk about it."

"I can see why."

She rolled her eyes. "Can we move past this?"

"I just want to understand how it works. Are you supposed to save me if I fall out of an airplane or get hit by a bus or something?"

"I can't undo death." The bleakness in her tone and the seriousness in her eyes were unnervingly genuine. "I'm an angel, not a god."

"So... you guard me from bad things before they happen?"

"I try to keep you out of danger, yes."

Something in her voice, in her face, had him almost believing her. Did that make him just as crazy as she was? He needed something that would settle the argument one way or the other. Something empirical. Inarguable.

He glanced around the tent, looking for something an alleged guardian angel might be able to protect him from. His gaze landed on a spare tent spike. That should be heavy enough to constitute "danger." He picked up the spike and held it over his bare foot. He turned it sideways, so as to minimize impact. "So... you'll keep me safe from this?"

He let go of the spike before she answered.

The flat side crashed into the top of his foot, sending a lightning bolt of shooting pain up his leg.

"Ow!" The spike rolled to a stop a few inches away. Sarah hadn't moved a millimeter. His foot was already starting to bruise. "You didn't save me from *that*."

She lifted a shoulder. "My job is to guard you from death, not from your own stupidity."

He stared at her for a long moment, his injured foot throbbing. Then he burst out laughing.

She was trolling him. *Obviously* she was trolling him. There were no guardian angels, just gullible travelers. She'd even gotten him to drop a metal spike on his own foot to prove her wrong. Next time, he wouldn't face her in a battle of wits until after he'd had a double shot of caffeine.

Still shaking his head at how easily he'd been had, he pushed to his feet and held out his hand. "Come on, angel. Let's go get some coffee."

CHAPTER 7

Three days later, the roofs were fixed and the frame was set for a small community center that could double as a church or school, whatever the locals needed. The problem was that was the *only* frame set.

No. Javier ran swollen fingers through his hair. That wasn't the problem.

The problem was the bridge.

Sarah was right about the bridge's instability and untrustworthiness. When he'd gone back in the daylight to orchestrate the piecemeal transfer of heavy materials, as he'd promised he'd do, he'd gotten an eyeful of reality. From the SUV, the bridge looked like a bridge. A *dangerous* bridge but, you know, a bridge. On foot, with the sides and underbelly at eye level, the bridge looked less like a bridge and more like a false-floor death trap. The locals didn't even dare cross the thing on horseback, which was one of the reasons they were so isolated and helpless.

They were also smarter than him. He could not believe he'd strutted across in an SUV and pulling a trailer. He couldn't even see how it was physically possible. Even if the weathered slats could somehow support the weight, the missing sections should've swallowed a tire, or sent him careening off the side.

He'd placed all the right phone calls, but the government was months away from sending help. He finally found a private company capable of replacing the bridge, but they were booked solid and couldn't break ground until after the rainy season, anyway.

Which meant triple the work and quadruple the frustration. He'd paid out the nose to find a team to run telephone and electricity lines, and there were the workers on the other side of the river, staring in disbelief at the joke of a bridge.

Obviously their trucks couldn't cross. They weighed ten times as much as the little trailer. The men could walk over, sure, but then what? Haul miles of cabling in thick coils on their backs? The company he'd hired to redo the village's poor plumbing had managed, but they hadn't needed to bring utility poles across the bridge. Or basket cranes. Construction equipment was much heavier than the SUV, even with an over-stuffed trailer.

All of which meant that for three solid days, Javier awoke long before dawn, scouted out territory, dreamed up plans, organized men, tromped through mud, shimmied up trees, scaled roofs, schlepped heavy equipment, mixed concrete, inhaled fumes, barked orders, watched out for children, rationed food, bandaged wounds, kept up morale, directed traffic, cut wires, hammered nails, bent pipes, and tumbled into his tent for a scant five hours' sleep before getting up and doing it all over.

He hadn't had a spare moment to even talk to Sarah, much less contemplate kissing her again. Not that she left him alone to this madness. She was everywhere he was, doing everything he was, always within earshot if he needed an extra hand. She was amazing, the villagers were amazing, the unexpected help from the neighboring towns was amazing, but what they really needed was... more.

The day after the hearing, Javier had liquidated his assets. He earmarked one third of the money for doing this exact sort of thing for the rest of his life. He donated another third to all the worthy causes he'd ignored during his years as a power-hungry mogul. He used the final third to start the nonprofit Rodriguez Foundation, with the goal of bringing relief to third-world countries and people in need throughout the globe.

Despite the full subsidization and grant money to anyone willing to donate a year of their time, the Rodriguez Foundation was unarguably Javier's least successful venture. The few volunteers he did have were stretched to their limits, and there were none to spare for a tiny village in the mountains of Bolivia in the last weeks of December.

Nonetheless, the faces around him were hopeful—possibly for the first time in years—and Javier was determined not to let them down. The villagers, like the majority of Bolivians, were Roman Catholics. They believed in goodness. And they deserved a Christmas miracle.

His bruised shoulders had helped haul the thick logs for the utility poles across the bridge and into town, and went back three more times until all the cabling had been brought across as well.

The men were busy holding poles and climbing ladders and running cable when Javier finally decided he could use a thirty-second break. He glanced around for Sarah and spotted her at the foot of an incline, gathering fruit with some of the local children.

He was so focused on *her* that he failed to watch where he was going, and his boot tangled in a nest of forgotten wire. He was bending over to try and untangle his foot when the rumbling began.

His first thought was *thunder*. His second thought was *earthquake*. His third thought was *Run!*

He caught sight of Sarah's terrified face and the screaming children pointing at something just behind him. Still struggling with the nest of wires, he glanced over his shoulder.

A stack of heavy utility logs had broken loose from the pile and was tumbling down the mountain directly toward him.

"Oh, *fuck.*"

Javier whipped his head back to his foot, frantically trying to loosen the wires enough to untie his trapped boot and hop one-footed down the mountain if he had to, but there was no way, no time, and nowhere to go.

When the shadows of the falling logs fell over his back, he glanced up at Sarah. At least she'd be the last thing he saw before he was crushed to death under seven-hundred-pound utility poles.

Her face was no longer terrified. If anything, she looked... confused?

She was doing the blinky-fluttery thing again, her face tilted not toward him, but toward his impending annihilation.

He braced for impact.

The first log bounced overhead, close enough to rustle his hair. The second log... didn't happen.

After several long seconds of absolutely nothing, Javier straightened his hunched spine and stared over his shoulder.

The utility poles had... *stopped.* Against all logic, against all gravity, against everything he'd ever learned from Bill Nye the Science Guy, dozens of heavy logs lay silent on the muddy incline, as harmless as tinker toys. Even the treacherous wiring entangling his feet had fallen aside like overcooked spaghetti.

He could walk away. He was *fine*.

He jerked his eyes back toward Sarah. She was looking at him, not at the death logs defying gravity just above him. Nor was she doing the epileptic fluttery thing anymore. If he had to put a word on it, he'd have to say she looked...

Guilty.

As if she'd made the impossible possible with just the power of her mind. As if she'd saved his life—no, "guarded him from death"—just as she'd promised she would. His lungs seized.

Holy mother of God. She *was* a guardian angel!

He scrambled out of the wiring as fast as he could and raced down the incline. His heart was still thundering from the adrenaline, from the fear, from surviving the freaking impossible. He grabbed her by the shoulders and tried to catch his breath.

"Did you do that?" he panted.

She didn't answer, but her cheeks turned a suspicious shade of pink.

"You *did* do it! I knew you did it! I mean, *are* doing it." He glanced over his shoulder. Yep, the utility poles were still defying gravity. A crowd was beginning to form.

As if she'd just realized what he meant, Sarah's eyes widened in alarm—then fluttered unnaturally.

The logs were once again on the move, but this time, not dangerously. The utility poles all but meandered down the incline, harmlessly coming to rest against this tree or that rock.

"You have got to be kidding me." Javier could barely even breathe, much less think. His heart was still in hyperactive arrhythmia. "You're an actual angel. You saved my life."

"All in a day's work," she mumbled, without making eye contact. "Keeping you safe is a full-time job."

He stared at her speechlessly. He was pretty sure his brain was going to explode at any moment. She really was an angel. A *guardian* angel. Which meant there *were* angels. His mind reeled. So did the rest of him. He had to sit down. No, he couldn't sit down. There was nowhere to sit. Plus, he was still gripping her shoulders. Why was he gripping her shoulders? Was gripping an angel's shoulders a sin? Oh shit, he'd *kissed* her. He couldn't remember anything in the Bible specifically being for or against making out with one's guardian angel, but AP Mythology had been pretty clear that god+mortal intermingling had never worked out for the Greeks. Or the Romans. Angel/human hanky-panky was probably an equally terrible idea.

He totally wanted to kiss her again, though. Right now. On the lips.

He shoved his hands into his pockets before he could sink them in her hair and further complicate what he'd believed was a very uncomplicated, temporary relationship. What had she said this morning? He'd slept on her *wing*. She had wings. Invisible ones. And he'd slept on one. Possibly drooled on it. Gallant.

The memory of their first encounter popped into his head. He'd run into an invisible wall and briefly seen stars. Not stars. *Wings*. He'd seen wings. He'd discounted them because, *wings*. And then she'd appeared out of nowhere. But it wasn't nowhere, it was right in front of him. The wings were hers. First he clotheslined himself on them, then he pinned her down and drooled on them. Why was she even still here? Guardian angel, sure, he got that, but she must have better things to do than get tackled and drooled upon. *Everyone* had somewhere to be for the holidays.

Oh God. The holidays! If anyone had epic Christmas plans, it would have to be an angel. The questions came so fast and so furious, he was practically speaking in tongues just to get them out.

"What are you doing for Christmas? Do you celebrate *noche buena*? Or is it more like heavenly Hanukkah? Are you right in the middle of a countdown? Or are you down on Earth because December isn't your thing? Do you guys do more of a Three Kings celebration instead, come January? Or are our dates so messed up it won't be holiday time for you until March or August? Oh, man, what if I'm off completely? It's incredibly presumptuous to assume my Sunday school lessons were the correct ones. Were the Greeks right, after all? The Romans? It would be badass if there really was a Medusa. Or Romulus and Remus! I already feel like I've opened Pandora's Box. *Is* there a Pandora's Box? Or a golden fleece?"

She inched backward. Slowly. And then blinked with careful precision. As if trying—and failing—to comprehend any portion of his exuberant babble.

"Never mind," he said quickly. "Don't tell me. It won't change anything, and I don't really need to know. The biggest miracle of all isn't that angels exist, it's that we've got one right here in the Bolivian jungle, right where divine intervention is needed the most. Can you magic the utility poles into place? Make sure everyone's wired up, maybe give them some 4G. It'll be awhile before the government can send anyone out here, and I really want these people to have a good Christmas."

She bit her lip. "No."

"And the bridge! They absolutely need a better bridge. And filtered water. And a pharmacy, or at least access to penicillin and—"

He broke off. Replayed her reply. Stared at her uncomprehendingly.

"I'm sorry, did you just say... no?"

She nodded infinitesimally. "I'm *your* guardian angel. Not theirs. I can only do miracles that directly affect you, and only when absolutely necessary to keep you out of harm's way. It's in my contract. You have a destiny. Everything else is... not my job."

An uneasy churning began to bubble deep in his stomach. *Not my job* were the last words he'd ever expected to hear from an angel. Perhaps they defined the term differently wherever she came from.

He pressed forward anyway. "Okay, you're assigned to me. Loud and clear. But you're obviously not the only guardian angel, right? If I've got one of my own, that means there's gotta be lots of you guys floating around. Right?"

She hesitated, then inclined her head. "There's a guild. But I'm a peon, not a powerhouse. I don't make the rules. I follow them."

"A guild! Right! Well, there you go. A heavenly guild of guardian angels. I hoped there was some sort of infrastructure to handle these things. I'm assuming you're here because I'm here, right? I mean here-here, not existentially. Bolivia. This village. That clipboard itinerary wasn't a coincidence. You were following me."

"Y-yes. I go where you go. But you're not supposed to see me."

"I'm not worried about that right now. I'm worried about these people, and their incredibly hard circumstances. Why aren't their guardian angels doing anything? They can't all be off fluffing clouds and playing harps. Shouldn't *they* be attending to the bridge and the roofs and the penicillin?"

"Hangottinny," Sarah mumbled without meeting his eyes.

The churning in his stomach twisted all the way into his throat. "I'm sorry, what?"

She kept her eyes averted. "I said, they haven't got any."

"Haven't got any what?"

"Guardian angels."

"None of them?"

She shook her head.

"Zero angels," Javier repeated. "Zero guardian angels in the whole godforsaken village."

"In... northern Bolivia," she corrected quietly. "It's a population thing. Angels are assigned based on destiny. There's some in Santa Cruz, several in El Alto, and a few in La Paz, but—"

"Are you shitting me?" he spluttered.

She was not. The misery on her face spoke for itself.

He couldn't believe it. "*This* is their destiny? No bridge, no roofs, nobody looking out. But a corporate shark with nothing but time and money on his bloodstained hands, *he's* the one who gets a guardian angel?"

"I know it doesn't seem fair. I'm not part of the planning committee, so I never saw the decision tree. But you have a destiny you were meant to fulfill. That's why my supervisors found you worthy. So do I." She bit her lip again. "And I've been watching over you since birth.

Long before you became a shark. Or a billionaire."

"No decision tree in the world should—" He sucked in a horrified breath. "Wait. *Birth?* Like, every minute of every day? Or just, like, sometimes?"

"Every minute of every day. Except during end-of-month reviews. Then I'm gone for a few hours."

Javier's blood drained. She'd seen him vomit up a pint of Jim Beam on his eighteenth birthday. She'd seen him spend three days in the bathroom after accidentally drinking the water in Morocco. She'd seen more than his deleted Internet history—she'd seen exactly how he reacted to that totally wrong, totally sexy, alien spaceship porn his college roommate had sent him.

There could not be a hole big enough to drown in right about now.

"But—the villagers," he said desperately. "Why don't they at least have a part-time angel watching over them?"

"There's a shortage," Sarah admitted.

"A shortage. Of angels. Are you guys in danger of extinction or something? Is it our fault? Do we need to stage a 'clap your hands if you believe in angels' viral video before the last ones die out?"

"No, we're basically immortal. It's just that there's a lot more of you than there are of us. And since it's basically confining yourself to an invisible solitary confinement for the rest of eternity, most magical beings choose a different career path. Like collecting children's teeth. Or coaching an interdimensional soccer team."

"Look," he said with as much patience as he could muster. "There's an angel shortage, and a need for miracles. You have the power to help these people. So, help them. What's the worst that could happen?"

"I'd be sacked," she answered immediately. "And then the world would have one less guardian angel."

He racked his brain. "What if I gave you permission? Dissolved whatever contract there is between you and me, so that you could help someone else *before* you get sacked?"

"Even if you could fire me as your guardian angel—which you can't—what about all the people who come after you? You may not be immortal, but I am. And the eternity of people who should've had a guardian angel but end up dying young because some billionaire with a hero complex decided he'd rather get his angel fired than let her continue watching over people... what about them? Are you willing to dissolve their contracts, too?"

His hands clenched into fists. "That's not a fair question."

Her smile was bleak. "You of all people should know the world isn't fair."

"So, what then? I just go about trying to save as much of the world as I can for the rest of my mortal life, knowing there's an invisible presence who *could* help out, but won't?"

"Not if I can help it," she said with feeling.

The first ray of hope pierced the gloom spreading inside him. "Really?"

"Of course. All this gallivanting around third-world countries is far too dangerous. What you *should* do is stay home."

The oxygen evaporated from his lungs. Months of improbable bad luck replayed through his brain. The inexplicable flat tires. The cancelled flights. The nightmares with Customs. The inability to rent cars or hotels or anything else he needed. The equally improbable reversal of fortune the moment he decided to head home. Direct flights with first-class beds. Limo chauffeurs on call. Zero traffic.

"*You* were responsible for the burlap sacks?" he asked inanely.

"No, I was responsible for the exploding luggage. I wanted you to go *home*. I still do. I've saved your life a dozen times since you landed, and barely a week has passed. If I'd seen the burlap sacks before you did, I'd have gotten rid of them, too."

Javier turned on his dirt-caked heel and stalked away before he came unglued.

She'd rather guard him from Starbucks spills back in Malibu than help him save children who needed miracles?

Well, too fucking bad.

Now that he knew she was contractually obligated to keep his ass alive, he planned to risk it as much and as often as necessary in order to keep improving lives. If she had to save him from falling logs and insurgent gunfire forty-six times a day just so he could keep making a difference, then so be it. Why *not* risk his life to save someone else's?

After all, he had a guardian angel.

CHAPTER 8

Sarah stared at the new community center without moving a muscle. Javier was on the roof, a power drill tucked into his waistband, as he teetered on the apex.

They hadn't spoken in days. Not that there'd been time for speaking. Javier had been far too busy throwing himself in harm's way at every possible opportunity. The projects were moving faster than ever, but if she so much as blinked, her stubbornly altruistic human was going to gore himself on his own drill. Or snap his spine falling off the roof. Or tumble headfirst into a pile of machetes. Or all of the above.

He'd been hard enough to protect when he hadn't had the slightest notion of her existence. Now that he knew the truth, it was almost impossible to keep him alive. She felt like *she* was the one balanced at the edge of a precipice. She needed to do everything in her power to salvage as much of the situation as possible before meeting her superiors. And now that her cover was blown, she really ought to go back to being invisible.

But she couldn't bring herself to do it. Not now. Not anymore. Why should she?

She was *so* fired at her end-of-month debriefing, it wasn't even funny. This would not only be her last assignment, it was also the last time she'd be allowed on Earth. They'd reassign her and wipe his mind and—

No. If she stayed as close to the spirit of the rules as possible, and avoided any flashy miracles, they might let her keep her position.

They might also erase her memory from Javier's mind which, after finally being *seen*, was more than Sarah could bear to think about. But being a guardian angel wasn't about one's own selfish wants. The human realm was already grossly understaffed. If they lost her, too… that would be the greater tragedy.

Much as she might like to miracle everything in this town, she could not risk a short-term fix costing the world another guardian angel for the rest of eternity.

So, here she was. Watching over Javier, and Javier alone. Doing her best to keep her job. And, perhaps, to keep *him*. At least until he turned seventy.

At the moment, he and most of the men from the village and the neighboring pueblos were hard at work patching up the death bridge with strips of wood and leftover roof bits and plenty of sun-bleached rope. He was currently hanging upside down, sinking counter-nails into the underside of the bridge.

Javier called it "pulling a MacGyver."

Sarah called it "madness."

He was so hardheaded and softhearted that she could barely look at him without her throat closing up and her lips curving with pride. He was magnificent. What he wanted, he got. What he wanted to do, he did. And steamrolled anything that dared get in his way.

And he was right, Sarah realized with sudden clarity. He didn't live according to arbitrary rules. He lived according to his heart. *He* was the angel.

In the centuries she'd spent on Earth, she'd watched over fourteen humans. Fourteen living, breathing miracles. She'd been glued to their sides from the moment of their births, and yet she couldn't claim to have saved a single one of their lives. She'd only kept them safe until the moment of their scheduled demise. That was their destiny.

She'd cried when death inevitably came. Every single time.

But that was the job. Without her, their lives would've been even shorter. She was a professional. A good one. And after going on a thousand years of service, she was watching over assignment number fifteen.

Javier? A baby. A blink in the eye of the cosmos. A momentary spark confined to a fragile human shell.

And he'd probably saved fifteen lives since breakfast.

He was atoning for sins he hadn't even knowingly committed, but Sarah knew him well enough to have realized long ago that his heart had always been wide open to others. Sure, one of the side effects of his company's rapid growth had been collateral damage to infrastructures or people or the environment. He wasn't wrong about that.

But he'd presided over his multibillion-dollar empire with a strong will and an even stronger moral compass. Despite subsidiaries and foreign branches sprouting up like gremlins, he hadn't permitted any of them to skirt any laws, to slip through any loopholes, or to take advantage of corrupt governments or delicate economies or a naive workforce. The same company in anyone else's hands would've destroyed far more than it created. After the hearing, the other businessmen had opened champagne bottles, not charities.

But Javier had become a one-man tornado. He'd reinvented himself as Captain Planet instead of Corporation King, and started funds and launched volunteer organizations and risked malaria just to lend a hand.

To her, *this* was why he deserved a guardian angel. Not to enable the corporate dynamo he had once been, but to encourage the global champion he now was. He was worth a thousand guardian angels.

Unfortunately, all they had was Sarah.

CHAPTER 9

After hammering in the last of the nails, Javier swung his gaze from the underside of the bridge to the crowd watching from the other side of the steep drop-off.

Even from this distance, even dangling upside down beneath slats of ancient wood, every fiber of his being was still painfully attuned to Sarah's. She was frustrated with him. He was frustrated with her. It was a standoff.

And probably futile.

The most annoying aspect of the whole mess —outside of her blind adherence to whatever ill-thought-out rule forbade her from helping anyone other than him—was that, despite it all, he still... *liked* her. She might be stingy with the miracles, but she was still omnipresent, ready to lend both hands at the first sign of need. She picked fruit, she shoveled dirt, she fed babies, she drilled holes, and she never flagged. She was amazing. Her maddening refusal to perform miracles just made everything else she did all the more incredible.

She was much more than just an angel. She was *Sarah.* A person in her own right.

And he was a dick.

With a grunt, he hauled himself back onto the correct side of the bridge and faced the truth. He shouldn't judge her when he didn't know the first thing about her.

Being pissed about her not breaking her corporate code of ethics just to please him was something Old Javier would've felt. New Javier was supposed to be all about walking a few miles in other people's shoes. He shot a surreptitious glance toward her feet and shuddered. Hopefully he wouldn't have to walk anywhere in astronautic orange-and-lime moon boots. Once was enough.

He doled out high fives and clapped sweat-drenched backs and herded his motley construction team off the newly MacGyvered bridge. It wasn't near strong enough for a cement mixer or heavy machinery, but it was sturdy enough to start busing kids to school.

The second he stepped off the last wooden slat onto firm land, Sarah's entire posture changed. Javier paused. He'd known she wasn't thrilled about his construction acrobatics, but he hadn't realized just how tightly wound she was until right this moment.

Her forehead cleared. Her fingers loosened. Her shoulders relaxed. He could practically *hear* her exhale the same breath she'd been holding since he first stepped onto the bridge. She didn't just worry about him. She was terrified she'd step away or blink her eyes for a millisecond too long, and in that time he'd fall to his doom. What had she said? *I can't undo death.*

She clearly meant it.

He'd been pushing her buttons on purpose, his already high risk-tolerance buoyed further by the safety net of a guardian angel. But she wasn't a safety net, was she? Life was the roller coaster and she was the guardrail. If he was stupid enough to vault over the railing, his messy corpse would be on his conscience, not hers.

Except that wasn't true, either. If anything happened to him—even if it were unquestionably *his* fault, not hers—Sarah clearly wasn't going to take it well. And here he was, making life harder. On purpose. Being a self-centered prick. He trudged up the bank to where she stood watch and wished he had a white flag of surrender to toss at her feet.

Or maybe roses. He'd bet it had been awhile since someone had given her flowers.

The apology he'd been about to make got caught in his throat, and what came out instead was, "Have you ever gotten roses?"

She stared at him as if a rosebush had sprouted right out of his head. He sort of felt like maybe it had.

"Roses?" she echoed blankly.

"Flowers of any kind. You know, like from a guy. To show he was interested."

Slowly, she shook her head. "I've never even been *visible* to a guy. Until you."

"I don't necessarily mean a human guy." He broke off, unsure now what he *had* meant. Or if he'd even thought it through. "Um... Do angels give each other flowers? Or is there some other heavenly courting ritual I can't even imagine? Cruising on cloud nine? Hiring a group of golden harp mariachis?"

She stared at him for a long, uncomfortable moment without so much as blinking.

"Good question," she admitted, softly. "If we do, I missed all that. Among the angels or otherwise. In school, I was considered a nerd. And as soon as I graduated from university, the Governing Council of Heavenly Beings recruited me. My first assignment was as a guardian angel, and that's what I've been doing ever since. Invisibility is a condition of employment. Not much opportunity for dating."

Javier could've slapped himself. Had he thought teasing her would erase the tension? He felt like an even bigger asshole than before. They'd already established she was the only guardian angel in the entire region. Who did he think would be bringing her flowers? Or courting her at all? When was she supposed to find time to go on dates? Or even have a moment to herself, to de-stress? Especially with an idiot like him, hanging upside down on a rickety bridge all day?

"I'm sorry," he said, finally finding the apology he'd meant to lead with all along. Although now it meant something different. Something worse.

He was no longer just apologizing for being embarrassingly pissy about her answering to a higher power rather than the desires of Javier Rodriguez. He was apologizing for the whole world, hers and his. He was apologizing for life itself, and how it wasn't fair for anybody. He was apologizing because she, of all women, deserved an infinity of roses. And so much more.

She glanced over his shoulder as if she hadn't heard him. "Bridge looks nice."

He snorted. That was a flat-out lie. The bridge looked like something Dr. Frankenstein's dog barfed up and Javier well knew it, but if she didn't want his apology, he wouldn't force it down her throat. But now that he'd thought of it, he couldn't get the idea of bringing her flowers out of his head. Or the sensation of paralyzing loneliness inherent in a job that required you to be literally invisible every second of your life.

His chest tightened. He still hadn't gotten used to the idea of being an unwitting client. The only other time he'd ever been an unwitting anything, he'd ended up a guest of honor at a congressional hearing. This was private, just between Sarah and him, but for some reason, it felt no less momentous.

The villagers had trickled away from the bridge. They'd headed back to work, to lunch, to their wives, to the next project. He and Sarah were alone along the bank of the river. Inches from the edge of a cliff.

He held out his hand. "Care to accompany me back to town?"

She stared at him without taking his hand.

His muscles froze. He kept his hand outstretched because he was too embarrassed to drop it. He was a moron. Obviously she would accompany him back into town. She was his guardian angel. She was—how had she put it?—contractually obligated to accompany him. On any fool mission he might dream up. Like it or not.

When was the last time she'd been able to decide anything for herself? To do something *she* wanted? Or to even be consulted?

He dropped his hand, heat crawling from the back of his neck all the way to his cheeks for probably the first time since sixth grade, when he'd sprung accidental wood at a girls' volleyball game. He felt no less self-conscious now.

"Sorry," he muttered again. "I realize you have to follow me, no matter what. But you don't have to hold my hand."

She slid her fingers into his, her voice almost too soft to hear. "I like to."

The rush of pleasure at those three little words was more than he deserved.

To distract himself from the sweetness of her fingers and the subtle scent of her hair, he hammed his way up the hillside, dramatizing every step and every groan as if they were weary hikers on the final stretch up Mount Everest.

"I'm getting old," he huffed, pulling a face. "I'm not sure these old bones can make it. What do you say, little lady?" He cast her an exaggerated leer. "Should we camp here for the night?"

That got a muffled laugh out of her. "Spare me. You're thirty-five."

"Exactly! And at our age—" He broke off as her true meaning sank in. Thirty-five would mean nothing to her. A hundred and thirty-five would be equally unimpressive. He was the billionaire playboy who'd never dated anyone out of her twenties, and she... "You're older than me."

It was a statement, not a question. By the look on her face, it was an observation she found much funnier than any of his attempts at charades.

"I'm older than everybody you know," she pointed out. "I'm an angel."

"How much older?" he found himself asking, although it patently didn't matter. "Like, on your next birthday."

The shadow that flickered across her pretty face immediately showed his mistake.

Either angels didn't celebrate birthdays, or

they *did,* except she didn't get to, because she was down here with him.

"When's the last time you were home?" he asked instead, more softly this time.

Her chin lifted, but her smile didn't reach her eyes. "Oh, all the time. Mandatory end-of-month debriefings, remember? Like clockwork. Every thirty days for almost a thousand years."

"That's not home. That's a board meeting with your boss." He tightened his hold on her hand. "When's the last time you were *home*?"

A glossy sheen coated her eyes and she quickly glanced away. "I don't have one. After a thousand years, you learn to think of 'home' as wherever you are, not where you'd like to be. Don't pity me. I'm not sorry I chose this path. I'm only sorry I might not be able to keep it."

"You'll lose your job because of me?" he asked quietly.

"Not because of you. Because of me. I knew the rules, and I broke them. I thought it was the right thing to do, but that doesn't make it legal."

"They'll know?"

"They'll *know*. You can't lie to the council of angels. If I'm lucky, maybe they'll let me come back. If I'm not lucky..." She waved this away. "Don't worry. Truly, I'll be fine."

"But if you won't have a job and you don't have a home," his runaway mouth blurted out, despite his better judgment, "then where will you go?"

She didn't answer. The tiniest, involuntary

hitch to her breath indicated she wasn't ignoring him. She didn't answer because there *was* no answer.

After a thousand years, there'd be no place to go home to.

"Let's not think about that," he announced, horrified he'd been insensitive enough to even bring it up. "Think about this: It's almost Christmas! A roof over our heads, Bolivian chilies in our bellies... we've got everything we could want. Except maybe a Christmas tree."

"I can't conjure one for you. That's outside my purview."

"I know," he said quickly. "I didn't mean—"

He stopped in his tracks, pulled her to face him. Her eyes were dull with resignation. His mind blanked in surprise, and his silver tongue failed to utter a single word.

It honestly hadn't occurred to him to beg her to miracle up some garish plastic tree, nor was he likely to criticize her if she refused to produce one. But how would she have known that? Here he was, trying to bring Christmas to the people who needed it most, and yet every time he interacted with Sarah, the only words that came out of his mouth were *me, me, me.* It was no surprise she expected him to ask for favors. He hadn't given her any reason to believe he saw her as anything more than a source of potential miracles.

His whole world tilted. If she'd never celebrated her birthday, it stood to reason she'd never had an opportunity to celebrate Christmas. Or Valentine's Day, or New Year's, or a prom, or losing her first tooth, or bandaging a skinned knee the first time she tried to ride a bike without training wheels. The only thing she'd ever had was a backseat view of other people's memories, while she remained confined to the shadows.

He couldn't give her back a life she'd never had, but the one thing he *could* give her was a week to remember. He took a deep breath. Here, now, gazing into the depths of her incredibly sad eyes, that one simple task seemed like the most important thing he could possibly accomplish. Christmas wasn't about getting, it was about giving. It was about family. It was about love. It was about *home*.

His guardian angel was the one person most in need of a miracle. And he would do anything in his power to make sure she got one.

CHAPTER 10

Sarah lay atop the sleeping bag and stared up into the shadows of the tent. Even if she'd been capable of sleep, she wouldn't have managed to get any. Not after Javier had turned her safe, ordered, black-and-white world upside down with nothing more than a fleeting look of pity.

Until she'd climbed that hill hand in hand with transitory mortal Javier Rodriguez, Sarah had actually believed herself to be pretty damn special. Superior. Enviable. Chosen.

While other inhabitants of Nether-Netherland struggled to find meaning, floundered for a purpose, dreamt of discovering a hidden talent for performing magic, Sarah Phimm had never suffered a moment's doubt as to her destiny or her place in the universe.

She'd been *born* with wings. She hadn't had to earn them in some complicated four-year recruitment process, or limp along on foot as so many others did. She could perform miracles. Not magic. *Miracles*. Could there possibly be a cooler innate talent than that?

No mind-deadening work at the pixie dust factory for her. Straight to the top. First day out of Uni, and she was already a guardian angel. Like any organization, the Heavenly Council had its red tape and its hierarchies, but Sarah had begun near the top. No internship, no apprenticeship—she was too good for that. Too special. Just *bam,* welcome to Earth, here's a helpless mortal baby. The next seventy years of its life are in your hands.

As a calling, guardian angelship was revered. Even among magical creatures. It trumped sandmen, dragon slayers, fairy godmothers. It was the highest position she could have possibly achieved, and it had been hers for almost a thousand years.

And for the very, very first time... she felt more than a little duped for having taken the job.

What if she *wasn't* the envied, exalted person she'd always imagined herself to be? How would she even know? As Javier had so world-shatteringly pointed out, her only interaction with others was during her end-of-month debriefing. A two-hour-long one-way conversation, wherein the only topic was Sarah.

Not exactly a global worldview.

What if the people she'd always looked down upon—the dreamcatchers, the tooth fairies, the license renewal clerks for magic carpet services —what if they looked down on *her*? What if they went home at night, to their families, their comfy chairs, their children, and looked at each other and said, "Poor old Sarah Phimm, stuck in that dead-end job. No friends. No home. Sure am glad I punch a time clock five days a week. Would sure suck to be on duty as some invisible ghost for the rest of eternity."

Or... what if they *didn't* say that? What if they didn't even remember her at all?

Maybe her superiors didn't remember who she was either, if her file wasn't right in front of their faces. After all, she was *a* guardian angel, not the only guardian angel. There might not be enough to go around for all seven billion of Earth's human inhabitants, but there were plenty enough to clog up the Heavenly Council's bureaucracy with meetings and TPS reports.

There had to be a better way. For her, and for every other angel out there, flying a mile in her feathers. She loved her job—she'd do it for an infinity of eternities if she could—but that didn't mean the system was perfect. Or that she was in any sort of position to do anything about it.

"Hey," came a soft voice from the pillow next to hers. "What are you thinking about?"

"Oh, you know," she answered blithely. "Weight of the world, impending apocalypse. The usual."

"None of that, missy. It's almost Christmas!"

Javier got to his feet and pulled her with him. "Less than three days to go, and we don't have a tree."

"We have lots of trees. We're in a rainforest."

"But they're not Christmas trees."

"How do you know?"

"They're not decorated." He lowered his lips to her ear. "The first rule of Christmas tree is: 'Thou shalt decorate the Christmas tree.'"

"That's the rule?"

"'Right after coffee.' That's the other part of the rule."

"Christmas depends on your coffee intake?"

"Everything I do depends on my coffee intake." His smile widened and the air in the tent seemed to disappear. "Well, almost everything."

Sarah held her breath, unable to tear her gaze from his. She thought maybe he was going to kiss her. She *hoped* maybe he was going to kiss her.

But then he threaded his fingers with hers and tugged her out into the warm glimmer of breaking dawn.

Once he'd replaced his blood with caffeine and had his morning shower, he gathered up a pack of supplies and dragged her deeper into the jungle.

"Palm, kapok, brazil nut..." he muttered as they ducked vines and leapt over leaf-cutter ants.

"What are you looking for?" she asked, after

the hike had stretched on for more than an hour.

"A tree! Aren't you helping? I thought your job was to pay attention."

"My job is to not let anything kill you. I'm not required to listen to botany monologues."

"A Christmas tree, Scrooge McAngel." He turned in a circle. "I'm going to have to give up on finding an evergreen, but I'm not giving up on St. Nick. You and the villagers are going to have a great Christmas, like it or not."

He turned and headed back the way they'd come.

Sarah hurried after him. "Where are you going? Aren't you going to cut down a tree?"

"No point, if there's no pine trees. These are the same kinds as over by the village. Might as well pick something that's already right there, if we're going to be stringing tinsel on palm trees."

"Are we going to be stringing tinsel on palm trees?"

"Somebody has to."

"Do Bolivians even decorate Christmas trees?" she asked.

"Not outside of the big cities," he admitted. "But that'll be a lot easier than whittling an entire nativity scene out of tree trunks. Especially since I don't know how to whittle. Now stop being a spoilsport. We have work to do."

They broke clear of the jungle canopy. Javier marched straight into the village—and then right out the other side. Sarah kept pace, mystified.

"Now where are we going? I thought you wanted a tree close to the villagers."

"Within sight of the villagers," he corrected as he came to a sudden stop. "Here. This is perfect."

"It... is?"

Javier stood before a flowerless deciduous tree with droopy green leaves and rough gray bark. Sarah had seen better-looking trees on animated Charlie Brown specials.

"Verawood?" she asked doubtfully.

"Bulnesia, if you want to get technical. *Palo Santo* in Spanish." Arms akimbo, he beamed at the thin-branched tree. "I'll have to fashion some sort of rain-proof platform for the gifts, of course, but we couldn't ask for a better location." He pointed back toward the village. "Perfect view from any of the houses." He swiveled ninety degrees to point in the direction of the bridge. "And perfect view for anyone entering the area. All we need now are some decorations. And some elves."

Now she *knew* he'd lost it. "Elves?"

"Not *elf*-elves. Obviously I mean children." His eyes widened and his jaw dropped. "It wasn't obvious? Are you saying there really are elves? Are there orcs? And hobbits?"

She sang out, "I'll never tell!" and raced him back into the village for supplies. In no time at all, they returned to the tree with two ladders, plenty of string, and every one of the children.

Javier pulled a long strand of silver-bell garland out of his backpack and let the kids lace it around the tree. He and the children sang carols as he helped them tie colored ribbons and brightly painted husks to the branches.

Sarah didn't sing along. She didn't know the words to "Burrito Sabanero." She didn't even know *Javier* knew the words to "Burrito Sabanero." That was another downside to watching someone listen to their iPod. Who knew what else she'd missed over the years.

Catching her melancholy expression out of the corner of his eye, Javier motioned to the closest children and whispered in their ears.

Sarah narrowed her eyes.

The children guffawed with delight and ran off in opposite directions, pink-cheeked and giggling.

Sarah's eyes narrowed further.

Javier flashed her a comically innocent smile and went back to work creating a mud-free platform out of bits of wood.

Not buying it, she crossed to where he knelt beneath the tree. "What did you just tell them?"

"I told them the story of mistletoe."

"That's why they were giggling?"

"They were giggling because I sent them off to find some."

"Does Bolivia even *have* mistletoe?"

"It doesn't matter," he answered solemnly. "At Christmas, it's the thought that counts."

"What kind of—"

He pointed overhead. A little boy who couldn't be a day over six lay draped over the closest branch, a purple-berried twig dangling from his tiny hands.

Sarah couldn't stifle her laughter. "That's *açaí,* not mistletoe."

"Christmas," Javier reminded her.

She smiled. "It's the thought that counts?"

"Absolutely."

He put down his tools and cupped her face with his warm, calloused hands. He lowered his head until his lips were barely a breath from hers. "Merry day before the night before Christmas, Sarah Phimm."

She slid her fingers into his hair and brushed her parted lips against his. "Back atcha, No Way José."

His mouth covered hers. The tree disappeared, the forest disappeared, the entire world disappeared. All that existed, all that mattered, was her and him, their mouths together, their hearts and breath as one.

The children's whoops of delighted laughter brought her back to reality.

She pulled away, cheeks flaming, lips tingling. "Build your fireplace mantel, Santa."

He grinned and went back to work on the small wooden platform. The raised base would keep the presents a safe distance from the ground, and the round-the-trunk design ensured the gifts would be visible from all angles.

She sat at the foot of a different tree to watch.

A split second of giggling was the only warning she got before an overhead branch dipped and another twig of dark-purple berries dangled over her forehead.

Javier immediately rose to his feet, as if he took this sacred duty very seriously indeed, and strode over to crouch beneath the giggling, trembling bough.

"This isn't even how mistletoe *works,*" she grumbled with mock Scroogery.

He kissed her anyway.

Even when he was done with the lower platform and had moved on to rain-proofing the top and wind-proofing the sides, he abandoned his tools and tasks and carols mid-word every time a handful of berries appeared anywhere near Sarah's head.

The kids loved it. *She* loved it, although she wouldn't give him the satisfaction of saying so.

She suspected he already knew.

The more he built up the makeshift mantel, the more he tore away at the walls around her heart.

How could she possibly leave this man? Her stomach clenched as an even worse thought occurred to her. Even if hell froze over and her rule-cleaving superiors somehow gave her another chance if she vowed to follow the rules, how could she possibly go back to living invisibly, silently, robotically, now that she knew what it was like to truly live?

Perhaps *this* was the real reason why the Heavenly Council never doled out second chances. Not because they held their angels to an impossible standard of perfection. But because no one would want it, after experiencing the wonders of imperfection.

She gazed at Javier. Love was everything she'd feared it would be. She blushed beneath his every heated glance and melted at the barest brush of his lips. He was silly and flawed and joyous and sincere and thoughtful and bullheaded and everything she could ever possibly want...

And could never have.

CHAPTER 11

The next day, Javier rounded up Sarah and all of the village children. He bundled the kids into the bus he'd procured for them—driven by one of the parents—and followed behind with Sarah, in the SUV.

Being as it was Christmastime, there'd be no classes until next year. Being as it was *noche buena,* this was his one and only opportunity to get presents under the tree before showtime. Especially since here, Christmas began on Christmas Eve, rather than Christmas Day.

Thanks to evening mass, the kids wouldn't be back until after ten. Javier intended to have the town tree overflowing with presents long before their arrival. He dragged the kids into every storefront the small pueblo had to offer, gauging their interest in various toys and measuring clothes against their small frames.

They had to stop earlier than he expected. Not because they ran out of time or money.

They'd run out of stores. He'd bought every toy and item of clothing even remotely suitable, and he was done shopping because there wasn't anything left to buy.

He'd likely also singlehandedly revitalized the local economy.

While the various shopkeepers set about gift-wrapping his thousand-and-one purchases, he took his troops for a stroll about town. Hand in hand, he and Sarah led the way across cracked or missing sidewalks, past a barbershop and a bakery, over a well-worn soccer field, through a mildly graffitied town square.

To kids who didn't even take nonleaking roofs for granted, it was nothing short of Wonderland.

They loved the school, with its crayons and books and cafeteria. They loved the church, with its lights and nativity and stained glass. They loved the park, with its concrete benches and trimmed grass and mosaic foun—

"Hey!" he shouted, sprinting toward them. "Don't drink out of the fountain!"

Too late.

The older kids had dipped their hands in, telltale wetness still clinging to their palms and chins. The smaller kids had pushed up on their toes, leaning their bellies over the side of the fountain to dunk their faces directly into the water.

The slightly murky, slightly oily, peppered-with-rusted-pennies-and-bird-droppings water.

"Oh, God."

The kids had stopped when he'd shouted, but Javier pulled them away from the edge anyway, as if mere proximity was a health risk.

Sarah jogged up beside him. "What's wrong?"

He gestured into the basin.

"They drank the water?" She recoiled. "Gross."

"Very. This water cannot possibly be healthy." He ran a hand through his hair. He sat down on the edge of the fountain, only to leap right back up. "I brought them here to give them some fun, not to poison them. Are they going to get sick? They won't die, will they?"

She blinked. Her lower lip moved speechlessly.

"Oh, right. You can't tell me, and you wouldn't help even if you could. Your miracles can only assist *me*." He didn't bother to mask the bitterness in his voice. He wasn't even sure he could. The "rules" might not be her fault, but that didn't make it fair. Or right.

He'd spoken to Sarah in English, but it didn't matter. The children were all staring up at him, round-eyed and nervous. One of them started to cough. Probably unrelated, he guessed, but still. Not good.

The oldest two—a girl and a boy who'd been coconspirators in the mistletoe game—seemed to be the only ones to put together the meaning behind his warning. The girl took a second glance at the water she'd been drinking and quickly turned away, as if nauseous. The boy laughed at her, but wiped the back of his hand across his mouth as if wiping away a taste gone sour.

Javier tried to think. Maybe they would be fine, and maybe they wouldn't. He was a billionaire, not a nutritionist, but he'd have to be blind not to see the potential for trouble. But what could he do? Sarah couldn't help him because of the stupid rules, and he was fresh out of magic wands to whisk away all his troubles.

Or was he?

He slanted a considering glance toward Sarah's concerned face. She *wanted* to help. He could see it in her worried expression, in the tightness of her shoulders, the way her fingers twitched as if itching to purify the water.

Well, he'd just have to make it easier for her to do so.

He sat back down on the edge of the fountain. "I'm going to drink some."

"Don't even think about it." She dug her fingers into his sleeve. "People *die* from contaminated water."

"Exactly."

Before he could change his mind, he plunged his cupped hands into the grimy water and raised them to his lips. She'd either have to purify the water supply or risk him catching whatever diseases it contained. He lifted his hands to his open mouth—

And choked in disbelief as orange-flavored saccharine coated his tongue.

Sticky wetness dripped from his fingers, splashing his khaki pants with pale orange drops. He jerked his head toward the fountain. It now brimmed with translucent orange liquid. Not a speck of dirt or grime in sight. He didn't have to take another sip to recognize the flavor.

He cast his angel an incredulous stare. "Are you freaking kidding me?"

"What?" she asked innocently. "You *like* orange Tang."

"I did when I was eight!"

She shrugged and lifted a palm. "*They're* eight."

"I thought you were just going to purify it."

"It's purified."

"I thought it would still be *water*."

The edge of her lips quirked. "What's wrong with a little flavor?"

"What's wrong with a nice Chianti?" he countered.

"No vitamin C," she pointed out. "Think of the children."

"I always do," he said quietly. "Are they safe?"

She sighed. "Never been healthier. I've neutralized every virus and germ in a ten-yard radius."

His shoulders sagged in relief. He looked over at the kids. They were crowded around the fountain, jostling and laughing, the moment of terror forgotten.

She'd saved them, despite the rules.

Not just that, he realized slowly, as the cascading towers of orange Tang glistened in the sunlight. The bigger miracle here wasn't that she'd saved the day, but *how* she'd saved the day. She'd hadn't just twitchy-eyed some clean water. His serious, rule-following guardian angel had actually had some fun with it. She'd done something *playful*.

He stared at her in astonishment... and love.

He should probably take her temperature, or check her for a concussion. He kissed her instead. Twice. And then another time for good measure.

The father who'd driven the children's bus stepped out of the row of shops and waved to let Javier know the presents were done being giftwrapped.

Javier glanced over his shoulder, trying to come up with a rational explanation for why the crumbling water fountain was now flowing with orange Tang, and blinked to discover that it wasn't.

Water flowed from all three levels, splashing into the basin below. Safe, clean, pure water.

"Tang you very much," he whispered.

She elbowed him. "Don't you have a chimney to slide down?"

Right.

He sent the kids into the church so they wouldn't see the presents being loaded into the SUV. And loaded. And loaded. There would barely be enough room to shoehorn him and Sarah inside.

He couldn't have been more pleased.

As soon as they were back in the car, he kissed the tip of Sarah's nose and turned the wheel toward the river. They had a solid four or five hours until the children would get back to the village, but Javier wanted to set things up sooner rather than later. Over the past week, the rain had gone from intermittent drizzle to an almost constant downpour, and the sky was once again turning dark and swollen. He wanted to get the presents safely situated before the heavens opened up and drowned them.

He glanced at Sarah and grinned to himself at her trick with the fountain. As soon as they'd decked the tree, he had some tricks of his own he'd like to show her. Preferably horizontally. And nakedly. Definitely nakedly.

Wait... what was he thinking? His fingers tightened on the wheel as a sudden doubt snaked down his spine. He had the one-in-a-million luck to get sent a guardian angel, and the first thought that occurs to him was boning her?

Not his *first* thought, he reminded himself piously. His first thought had been saving the children. His *second* thought had been taking the angel to heaven.

He downshifted over some rough terrain. Probably there was a special place in hell for people like him. A special room called "Egocentric Assholes Who Performed Unholy Acts with

Guardian Angels." Probably guys like him were exactly why the powers that be were so stingy with assigning angels in the first place. Probably just the fantasy alone was more than enough to ensure a nice toasty afterlife.

Didn't stop him from wanting her, though.

He slid another glance her way and faced the truth. He would never stop wanting her. He was throwing every fiber of his being into creating the Best Christmas Ever because he couldn't bear to contemplate what would happen afterward.

She'd lose her job, she'd said. Even if she didn't, it didn't take a genius to realize they'd never trust her alone with him again. He figured he'd pretty much lost all guardian angel rights the first time he'd kissed her. His skin went clammy.

Being on his own in one sense didn't bother him in the least. He hadn't even known he *had* a guardian angel until just recently, so it wasn't like he would miss having an invisible, wordless entity shadowing his every move.

What he *would* miss... was Sarah. His stomach twisted upside-down just thinking about it. Which was why he wouldn't think about it.

He would think about tonight, and the next night, and the next night. He would think about the time they still had left, not the eternity they would be apart. He only wished he'd been able to appreciate the thirty-five years they'd had together before he'd been clued in. And honestly, could there be any greater proof that she was the perfect woman for him than that? She *knew* him. She knew him better than anyone ever had or could.

She knew every tiny secret he'd tried to hide from others, every humiliation he'd tried to block from his own mind, every success and every failure, every joy and every sorrow. And she liked him anyway.

He grinned at her. She crossed her eyes and stuck out her tongue. He grinned wider.

An eternity together wouldn't even be enough.

CHAPTER 12

By the time the last of the presents was tucked safely behind the clear plastic curtain encircling the tree, Sarah's sopping-wet hair was matted to her skull and her sodden clothes felt like she was enshrouded in papier-mâché.

None of which had stopped Javier from searing her with swift, molten glances that thrilled her all the way to her toes. She was half-surprised the rain wasn't evaporating off of her as steam.

Javier was equally as drenched, and far sexier than any human had a right to be. His dark hair stuck to his forehead, his T-shirt clung to his chest and biceps, his pants were soaked to the skin—and Sarah had never seen him look hotter.

She wanted him. Not in a back-of-her-mind, secret fantasy sort of way. Not anymore. Now it was an all-consuming, breath-stealing, heart-racing, soul-baring *need*. To feel him next to her. Inside her. To hold him, to *have* him. To let him know she was his, body and soul, till Heaven did them part.

He stepped closer, away from the tree. She held out her hand, expecting him to lead her back to the tent. He didn't. He ignored her hand, choosing instead to grab her to him and swing her in an exuberant circle, as if he'd finally been granted his heart's desire.

"The kids?" she guessed, laughing as he twirled them beneath the rain. "You're happy you managed to bring them a Christmas?"

"You," he corrected gruffly, and claimed her mouth with a kiss. "You *are* my Christmas."

She couldn't respond—didn't have the words to respond, would never have the words to describe the thundering in her chest—but before she could do more than try to show him with her eyes all the love she held in her heart, his hands cradled her face and his lips covered hers once more.

She opened her mouth, opened her arms, opened her heart. *This* she could respond to. This didn't require words, didn't require thought. It was pure feeling. Primal. Two people, two bodies, two souls. Poetry at its most powerful. Hearts at their most vulnerable. She wrapped her arms around his neck and hung on for dear life.

The rain covered them, bathed them, pelted them. She barely noticed. His lips were firm and warm and tender, his tongue as intoxicating as honey wine. He lifted her, and she wrapped her legs around his waist. Her thighs encircled the curve of his leather belt, her core flush against the hard ridge beneath his zipper. His hands cupped her behind, pulling her to him even more tightly.

He needn't have worried. She was never letting go.

He kissed her as if he were drowning, as if her lips were the only source of oxygen, as if her tongue emptied his head of everything except the desire to be even closer. She had nothing in her own head except his scent, his taste, the delicious sensation of his hot tongue and hard body beneath the onslaught of cold rain.

She poured every atom of her being into the passion driving her kiss. Her heart pounded against his, twin drums in the night. A thousand years of loneliness had led her right here, to him, to this perfect moment. She never wanted it to end. Would die if it did.

She tore her mouth from his only long enough to pant, "The tent?"

"Absolutely." The wicked promise in his eyes enflamed the embers of naked want cleaving her to him.

She wasn't sure she could release him long enough to *make* it back, much less force her trembling legs to walk.

When her reluctant feet were back on solid ground, he laced his fingers with hers and pointed toward the tent. "First one there gets to strip the other one naked."

She grinned and took off running, her hand in his, both of them racing through the mud and the night with rain sleeting down their faces and a fire burning out of control between them.

Javier caught her around the waist as soon as they reached the tent. His arms warmed her, his mouth seared her, as if the few seconds of having only their clasped hands connected had driven him mad with the need to have her in his arms once again.

Without breaking the kiss, without lifting his warm mouth from hers for even a second, he reached for the closure keeping the tent safe from the storm. He tugged at the zipper, once, twice, again, and then they were tumbling into the opening, bringing with them the night and the rain and a storm of their own making.

He zipped up the closure, blocking out the weather. Kneeling, he reached for her in the dark. She stopped him, her lips to the sensitive skin beneath the base of his ear.

"Leave the skyward panel cracked open."

His lips sought hers. "We'll get wet."

"We're already wet."

"You'll get cold."

"You'll keep me warm." She cupped his cheek, touched her lips to the corner of his mouth. "I want to see you. To know you can see *me*. I don't want to be invisible. Not tonight."

His tongue met hers as he opened the zipper

overhead a few inches, letting in the rain and the night air and the flashes of lightning. The night smelled like clean grass, like tropical flowers, like paradise on earth. But all she could smell was *him*.

All she could see was him. All she could *feel* was him. His hands, his breath, his body, closer than she'd ever dreamed. More solid and real than anything she'd ever known. More precious than anything she'd ever desired.

She reached for his T-shirt, rolled the wet cotton up over his stomach, up over his chest.

"Hey, I thought *I* won the race," he teased, but he lifted his arms.

She nipped his lower lip. "And now it's time for your prize."

He grinned. She winked and continued removing his shirt. The storm eased slightly, and hints of moonlight began to filter through the falling rain.

He let her push the wet cotton up over his triceps, over his head, over his wrists, in silent understanding that this inch-by-inch unveiling wasn't meant to torture him, but instead was a gift to herself. The gift of touching, of *connecting*. Of mutual desire.

He was perfect, of course. As she'd always known he would be. But knowing and seeing were totally different from touching and tasting for herself.

She tossed the sodden shirt aside and pressed her lips to his chest. He should be cold, but his skin was hot, just as hot as her own. She dragged her open mouth to his nipple, flicked her tongue against the taut nub. He flinched. She smiled. He tasted like rain. Fresh and pure. He smelled of sandalwood and stardust. A little bit like her. A thrill of possession heated her blood. Quickened her pulse.

He lowered his arms to his sides. She slid her hands along his forearms, up his biceps. Her fingers were shaking. Not from the cold. From the heat.

She straddled his lap, sinking her fingers into the wet silk of his hair as she pressed her mouth to his. The rain was slowing. Soon, stars would light the sky. But nothing could dazzle her as much as being here, with him. The night was already perfect. She kissed him again, reveling in the sensation of his warm muscles beneath her fingers.

He reached for the hem of her shirt. She zapped it—and the rest of her clothing—back into the ether from which it came. She kept her wings invisible, too. Tonight was about her and him.

His hand slapped her now-bare ass. "Cheater."

"It wasn't real." She was fiercely grateful for the faint moonlight, thrilled beyond measure to be saying these words aloud, face to face. "I don't want you to make love to an illusion, or even an angel. I want you to make love to *me*. Who I really am."

"You're all I want." His words were a soft breath against her ear seconds before his warm mouth pressed a lazy trail of soft kisses down the curve of her neck.

She didn't feel naked anymore. She felt invincible.

His head lowered. The trail of slow, spicy kisses started their descent from the flat planes of her collarbone to the gentle slope of her breast. She luxuriated in the sensation, torn between pressing her naked chest to his and arching her spine, allowing him even greater access.

She opted for arching. He rewarded her instantly.

His tongue swept across her upthrust nipple, eliciting a moan of pleasure from deep inside her throat. He cupped her breasts in the palms of his hands, bringing first one and then the other to his open mouth to suckle.

The rough surface of his tongue and the wet heat of his mouth sharpened the ache of desire pooling between her legs. Her pulse thundered erratically. Her core throbbed. She needed him out-out-*out* of his pants, of any obstacle between them. She needed to see him, to feel him. All of him. Sliding within her.

She fumbled with the buckle of his belt. Partly because in this position, with her back to the sky and her legs tight around his hips, she couldn't see what she was doing. And partly because the barrage of sensations threatened to overwhelm her. The edges of her knuckles rubbed against the hard outline of his arousal. The fingertips of her pinkies brushed against her own wetness. She was wound so tight, she couldn't even think.

His strong hands caressed her trembling fingers. Deftly, he released the stubborn button, lowered the straining zipper.

She scrambled backward, abandoning his lap to prop herself up on her elbows, giving him space to rid himself of the offending barriers between them. He shucked his boots and pants and boxers, but when she reached for him, he did not let her rise.

He knelt between her legs, his hands warm against the cool gooseflesh dancing up her thighs. His head lowered. He kissed the inner curve of her knee, then the sensitive flesh along her inner thigh.

There was no doubt where these kisses were heading, no doubt at all what he intended to do once he got there, but he took his sweet time moving from lower to upper thigh, as if no portion of her skin was to be savored less than any other.

To her surprise, she wasn't nervous. She was *greedy*. Her entire body tingled, not just the parts he touched. Every inch trembled in anticipation. She wanted him to hurry. She wanted him to go slow. She wanted everything, all of it, every possible permutation, because the night would not last forever and she wanted to experience it all, here, with him.

She intended to stay on her elbows, watching the play of moonlight on his hair as he spun magic with his sinful mouth. But the moment his tongue finally, *finally,* licked the proof of her desire straight from her core, her elbows turned boneless and her shoulders melted into the floor. She gasped his name.

Her entire body had turned to jelly, but not her insides, not the inferno of need and want swirling to a crescendo she hadn't even believed possible. Seeing is one thing, hearing is another thing, but *feeling*... feeling was everything.

The pressure built and built until she was certain she would die from the delicious pain of it, the beautiful suffering, the glorious anticipation, the heady dizziness of teetering on the brink, on the cliff, on the—

She cried out as the waves broke through her. Her head lolled, her fingers twitched, her thighs tightened around his head, as his heavenly tongue coaxed more sensation from her than she'd ever known existed. Her toes clenched and unclenched, mirroring the rhythm of the orgasm wracking through her, until at last she lay limp, not capable of anything more.

He lay next to her, pulled her into his arms. She was too languid to do much more than curl into him. Distantly, she expected pressure of a different sort, a continuation of the show, of the pleasure. Instead, he simply held her close, his lips to the top of her head.

When the aftereffects of mindless ecstasy had settled into mere euphoria, she raised her head and smiled at him. She didn't need the aid of stars to sense he was smiling back at her. Had probably *been* smiling for the past five minutes.

She poked him in the chest. "I'm not done with you, mister."

"Thank God." But he made no move to pin her beneath his long, lean body and finish what they started. What her insatiable flesh was already clamoring to continue. How much lovelier would a climax feel with him inside of her, their bodies joined as one?

"Well?"

"Well, what?"

"Aren't you going to..."

He waggled his brows. "Ravish you?"

She frowned. "Don't you want to?"

"For the rest of my life," he said with feeling. "But I don't have to race to the finish line on the first night. I plan to savor our time together for as long as humanly possible."

Well, wasn't that sweet. Sarah pursed her lips and tried not to show how frustrating sweetness was, when what she really wanted was some good old-fashioned sexing.

He touched her cheek. "I'm not going to rush you. You haven't gone out on a date for an entire millennium. You're on a different clock than I am. I can respect that."

She was definitely on a different clock than he was. Her clock was set to *now*. She'd lived long enough to know that no matter how long you lived, it was never as much time as you hoped. Time had a funny way of stretching on forever, and then being suddenly over when you least expected it. She planned to savor every moment with him, too. And she planned to savor it by not wasting what little they had left.

She trailed her fingertips up his chest. "So... I set the pace?"

"You set the pace." His eyes twinkled. He held out his arms as if they were bound by chains and raised his voice with dramatic flair. "I am yours to command, O mistress of my fate, O siren of the night, O nymph of the—"

She swatted his arms. "Enough with the theatrics, Shakespeare."

He kissed her hand.

"I *am* yours," he said quietly. "It's both as dramatic and as simple as that."

She stared at him. He gazed back at her. He wasn't teasing.

"I'm yours, too," she whispered, even softer than the wind.

His grin was nothing short of cocky. "I know."

She dipped her head to nip that cocky smile. It only made him smile wider.

She smiled right back. Mr. In-control-of-everything-and-everyone wanted her to take charge, did he? Now *that* was something she could work with.

He might think of her as a thousand-year-old virgin—and, strictly speaking, he'd be right—but the world had come a long way over the course of that millennium. She'd been right there watching. Sarah was no sheltered miss, unclear on the mechanics of lovemaking. He might consider himself something of a renaissance man, but she'd had a front row seat to the actual Renaissance. Including its nocturnal activities.

She walked her fingertips down his chest, down his abs, down to... *yes*. Exactly here.

Javier sucked in a shallow breath.

Despite her knight errant's sincere intention of taking it slow, his cock had—luckily—missed the memo. It had been eager and rock hard from the moment they hit the tent and, if anything, had only gotten bigger. She curved her fingers around its rigid length, marveling at its heat, its strength, the way it reacted to her touch almost as if it had a mind of its own.

"Sarah—"

"Shh. I'm setting the pace."

She lowered her head. His hips arced upward the moment he felt her mouth join her fingers. She stroked him with her hand as she tasted him on her tongue. His entire body tensed. The rain was barely falling, and the only sounds filling the tent were Javier's rapid breathing and the wet suck of her mouth on his cock.

Without lifting her head, she rose on all fours and twisted until she could see him from the corner of her eye. His eyes were dark, his face pale, his lips dusky red. He was watching her as if she were a wet dream come to life, a miracle in the flesh.

Without lifting her lips, she met his eyes and smiled.

His hips jerked and he groaned in pleasure.

"You might want to stop setting such a good pace," he gasped hoarsely. "I might've been wrong about not racing to the finish line."

With a final lick from base to tip, she began a series of open-mouth kisses from his navel to his abs, from his abs to his chest, from his chest to his jaw.

He grabbed her with both hands and brought her mouth to his, delivering a crushing, searing kiss that thrilled her from her racing heart to her curling toes.

Loving the passion of his kisses, the taste of their tongues together, she swung one leg over his hips until she straddled his jutting cock. She rubbed against it. He didn't let go. Instead, he deepened the kiss.

She wriggled into place, lifting her head only long enough to reach down and guide their bodies together.

This time, it was *she* who gasped.

She could never have anticipated the quickening—the fullness—the spiraling arousal—the *rightness* of being locked together with him in body as well as heart.

His hands were now at her hips, gripping, guiding, kneading. His mouth found her aching nipple and she cried out, her back arching in pleasure. She rocked her hips, her pelvis rising and falling, his mouth to her breast, her pulse racing as that glorious pressure began to build yet again, building, building, building with every thrust, every suckle.

I love you, she wanted to say, but didn't. Couldn't. She was overwhelmed with *feeling,* with sight and smell and taste and touch, and didn't have room in her tumbling thoughts to contemplate anything more.

He grinned up at her as if he'd heard her, anyway. As if he didn't need words to be spoken aloud for them to pass from her heart to his.

The pressure burst and she shattered, her mouth open, her muscles clenching tighter and tighter, riding out the tidal wave of pleasure. He joined her, his breath just as shallow, his kisses just as desperate, his tongue just as hot, driving into her with his body and melding with her heart.

She slumped forward, spent, too weak to lift her face from his chest, too sated to bother untangling their limbs. His heart thundered beneath her ear, loud and strong and steady, and her eyes drifted closed.

She felt his lips in her hair, a kiss held at the top of her head. She felt the gentle puff of his breath, a breeze so slight it was almost indeterminable, and the words he whispered so softly into her hair she almost hadn't caught them: *I love you.*

She smiled. She would love him forever.

CHAPTER 13

Javier could've spent the rest of the night—no, the rest of his *life*—lying there naked with Sarah in his arms. But they didn't have that luxury. And besides, both of them were on the job. Tonight was *noche buena,* and Christmas Eve wasn't about what Javier Rodriguez wanted. The blinding glow of his smartphone indicated they had maybe twenty minutes to get up, get dressed, and get to the tree before the school bus came chugging back over the bridge.

Nothing was better than hot sex with the woman you loved, but playing Santa was definitely a close second.

He grinned. Santa and *Mrs.* Claus.

"Get up, get up!" He tugged Sarah's hand until she let him pull her to her feet.

Whereupon she promptly collapsed against him. "What's with all the energy? I thought real men could be trusted to fall asleep afterward. My illusions are shattered."

He kissed the bridge of her nose and knelt to rummage through his backpack. Big red pants, shiny black belt, bigger red coat. He tugged on his black hiking boots.

"You've got to be kidding me," Sarah said without bothering to hide her laughter.

Just for that, he popped the white-trimmed red hat on *her* head instead of his. She looked fetching. Mega fetching. Festive hat, naked body was definitely a good look for her. How much time did the phone say they had? Surely they could spare a few moments for a quick—

She pulled off the hat and snugged it down on his head. Before he could complain, her eyes did the blinky-fluttery thing and she was suddenly fully clothed.

Fully clothed as in, wearing the exact Santa's-helper costume Zooey Deschanel had worn in *Elf*.

Javier smiled wolfishly. He liked. Oh yes, he liked.

She wagged her finger in warning. "None of that until later, buddy. And only if you're a very, *very* good boy."

He would be anything she wanted.

"Come on, we have to hurry." He tugged her out of the tent and onto the trail. The rain had stopped, but the sky was still dark. "I want to be there to see their faces when they catch sight of the tree."

They jogged hand in hand down the dirt path, a perfect mirror reversal of their race to the tent a few hours earlier.

He felt like a completely different person now. He'd tried so hard over the past two years to become New Javier, a man driven by philanthropy, not greed, whose bottom line was number of lives saved, not number of companies owned.

He hadn't been New Javier, though. He hadn't been any Javier at all. He'd been directionless and lost, a shadow of his old self, a man seeking a purpose, a destiny, anything at all to keep him from falling apart.

And with one misstep, with one flying clipboard and a glimpse of impossibly bright wings, his world had changed forever. He'd found life again. He'd found Sarah.

He squeezed her hand, unwilling to let go even for a second, but the wind and rain had managed to glue bits of mud and leaves to the clear plastic lining protecting the presents from the elements. The kids would be coming around the corner any minute, and he wanted them to have an unobstructed view of the gifts that awaited them.

He picked leaves off the plastic lining as quickly as he could, but there wasn't much he could do about the streaks of dirt and mud. He motioned Sarah to go ahead.

"Go stand at the intersection. Let me know if you see them coming."

She stood her ground, clearly as unwilling to leave him as he was to leave her. "I can see the bridge from here. It's far, but it's not that far."

"We can see the bridge, but we can't see the road leading up to it because of the curve. By the time we see the bus, they'll already be here. If you're close to the river, you'll see them early enough to give me a warning shout."

"So that you can do what, exactly? Swoop out of the sky with your miniature sleigh and eight tiny reindeer?"

"Nine," he corrected her solemnly. "Don't you recall... the most famous reindeer of all?"

She gave him a quick kiss on the lips. "That's my cue to back away slowly before you burst into song."

"I thought you liked my singing!" he protested as she sauntered off.

Her voice carried over the wind. "You call that noise singing?"

He burst out laughing. "You're not a very nice angel!"

She stuck out her tongue and kept walking.

He loved that tongue. He loved *her*. As soon as Christmas was over, they were going to have to put their heads together and figure out a way to—

His hand flew out and braced against the tree trunk for support as the ground shook beneath his feet.

What the hell was that? Earthquake?

He jerked his gaze toward Sarah. She was

maybe a hundred yards away, closer to the bridge than to him, wearing an equally baffled expression. He motioned her on.

If it was a tremor, it was over now. It had barely lasted a second. Thank heavens. That was the last thing these people needed. They'd just gotten their roofs patched, for God's sake. He'd done his personal best at giving them rainproof roofs, but there wasn't much he could do to make ramshackle houses earthquake-proof.

He turned back to the circle of presents and resumed picking leaves off the plastic lining. His boots sank deeper and deeper into the mud, as if the weeks of rain had turned the rainforest into quicksand.

As if on cue, a crack of thunder rent the sky and the first cold wet drops splattered on his face.

Great.

"They're coming!" Sarah shouted from her vantage point along the river's edge. Despite the hard time she'd given him earlier, her eyes were shining and she bounced on her feet in obvious excitement. She might burst into song even before he did.

"Roger that!" he called back, lifting up his foot to edge around to the other side of the tree.

Tried to, anyway.

He frowned down at his feet. The toes of his boots weren't even visible anymore. It looked like his feet started at the ankle. With superhuman effort, he managed to pull his right boot up out of the sucking dirt, then the left boot. If he'd been wearing tennis shoes, he'd have lost them completely.

Another rumble shivered beneath the soil. He shot a quick glance over at Sarah, to make sure she was safe.

She was fine. Hadn't even noticed. Was too busy gazing down the river and clapping her hands in glee.

A shadow fell on the wet earth stretching between them.

He glanced up at the sky. Filtered moon, hidden behind the clouds. Trees, vines, nothing that could cause such an enormous, perfectly round shadow. The rain began to fall harder.

He squinted, trying to make sense of what he saw. The shadow was growing larger. Darker. And faster. He realized what it was the same instant the earth fell away.

Sinkhole.

"Sarah!" he screamed, but there was nothing to do, no way to warn her. It had already happened.

Ninety of the hundred yards between them disappeared into a perfectly round chasm. He couldn't see the bottom, didn't want to step away from the safety of the tree to even try.

His boots were covered again. Up to his ankles. Higher this time.

Sarah whipped toward him, eyes wide as harvest moons, just as the bus rounded the corner. She couldn't see it because she was facing him, and the driver couldn't see anything at all because of the dark and the mud and the rain, but Javier had a horror-perfect view of the imminent disaster. The sinkhole was too close to the steep drop-off to the river. The weakening ground would cause a landslide at any moment.

Already, this side of the bridge was sliding, sliding, sliding.

And the bus had just lumbered onto the other side of the bridge.

Sarah started sprinting in his direction, unaware of the nightmare unfolding behind her. Javier made slashing gestures with both arms, signaling her not to come this way, but she was heedless of his warning—or the danger to the children.

"Kids!" he screamed, pointing emphatically behind her. "Go get the kids! I'm fine!"

She paused to glance over her shoulder and stopped in her tracks. The bus was getting closer. Closer to its doom. She turned back to him. "You swear you're safe?"

"I'm great, I swear!" He wasn't great. He could already feel the ground shifting beneath his feet. But he was the one who bought the bus, who sent the kids across the river for Christmas mass, knowing they would be making the return trip after dark. She *had* to save them. No matter what.

Sarah hesitated, clearly torn. She didn't want to let him out of her sight—Lord knew, she had good instincts—but the bridge wasn't going to hold for much longer. Not with the ground beneath it sliding into the river below.

"I don't know what to do." Her voice shook. It was the first time he'd ever heard her say *I don't know*. Maybe the first time she'd ever felt indecision. Her life had always been black and white, good and evil, rules and commandments. She glanced behind, saw the bus had already come too far to turn around, the bridge too imbalanced to hold for more than a few more seconds. The kids already screaming, terrified. Fear laced through him. "Javier, I—"

"I love you, too!" he shouted back, motioning for her to hurry. "Save the children!"

With a final tortured glance in his direction, she turned and flew—literally *flew*—to the teetering bus, just as the bridge disappeared beneath it.

It was the last thing he saw before the ground opened up beneath him and swallowed him whole.

CHAPTER 14

Sarah concentrated every feather of her being on holding the bus steady. She'd gotten there in time to save the children from falling, but it was going to take all her focus to *keep* them safe.

There were too many variables, too many unknowns. The bridge was gone, which was actually one less thing to worry about, but the bus was packed to the gills with a dozen sobbing children and one terrified father who didn't seem the least bit comforted at being suspended in midair over a forty-foot drop filled with jagged rocks and a deadly current.

She would've already set the bus down safely, except she couldn't *find* anywhere safe, couldn't seem to do *anything* safely. The shore had fallen into the river, and what was left of the road was already chasing the rain down into the currents.

And now instead of having one soul to keep safe, she had thirteen. Thirteen personalities she didn't know, thirteen sudden movements she couldn't predict. Thirteen precious wildcards that she needed to get to safety as soon as possible so that she could go protect Javier.

She was going to have to set the bus down on the far side of the river, on the side they'd just come from. It was the only way.

No. Bad idea.

Separating the children from their mothers, from their frantic, panicked families, would cause much more harm than good.

But what was she supposed to do, then? Fly them to safety in the middle of the village? Who did she think she was, Superman? Toast of the *Daily Planet*? She was no hero. She was a very scared, very solitary angel who had broken every rule she'd sworn to uphold in order to save the lives of the people inside this bus.

Screw it, she was flying them to the village, even if it cost her job. Sarah *couldn't* let them die. The Heavenly Council could deal with their memories later. She flapped her wings. Time for a true miracle.

While the bus was levitating relatively safely, she stabilized the sides of the river as best she could. She couldn't undo time, but she could stop the landslide from getting worse. And more.

Maybe she didn't need to fly beneath the bus in her elf costume and best Superman pose, but hey. It was Christmas.

But now that the bus was safe on land, there

was no extra time for holding hands and drying tears. Javier was still out there. As long as he'd held on to that tree...

She missed it at first, because she couldn't find her landmark. Any landmark.

Couldn't find the tree.

Couldn't see Javier.

She saw the sinkhole, obviously she saw the sinkhole, but it wasn't like *Javier* was in the sinkhole, no, nothing like that at all. She'd *seen* the sinkhole, and seen Javier safely on the other side, right there next to the tree with all the presents.

So where the hell was he? And where the *hell* was the tree?

It wasn't a big tree, okay, sure. It was a small tree. Slender tree. Unassuming, really. Nothing special. Except it was *very* special. It was the Christmas tree, the one the kids had helped decorate, the one the presents were under, the one where Javier had teased her with the mistletoe.

It couldn't be *gone*.

She flew around, and around, and around, and almost didn't see it because of the rain or the tears or whatever was in her eyes, but there was a sparkle in the mud, a definite sparkle, something... something sparkly and Christmassy and joyous, something that shouldn't be buried in the mud at all.

She dropped like a stone, landed hard. She dug in her hands, flinging mud and dirt over her shoulders like a wild thing.

Silver bells. Tiny bells, long strand. Javier's garland for the Christmas tree.

She didn't even recognize the mewling, haunted whimpers coming from her throat. She had to dig. Where there was garland, there were presents. Where there were presents, there was Javier.

There had to be.

Her shoulders ached, but it didn't matter. She'd dig until her arms fell off if she had to.

She would've miracled up a shovel except she didn't want to risk hurting him, with no way to know how close he might be to the surface, or if he was hurt. He better not be hurt. She'd kill him if he was hurt. She dug with her hands because it was safer for Javier, even if her fingernails were torn and her knuckles bled freely. She couldn't even feel it. Couldn't feel anything, except a great yawning emptiness where there used to be light.

His hand. She'd found his hand!

Dirt flew until his hand was in hers at last. His fingers were cold, too cold.

No, no, not *too* cold, she assured herself. Of course they were cold. Obviously he was cold. She herself was chilled to the bone, to the soul, shivering and shaking as if she'd never be warm again. His fingers weren't shaking. They were stiff.

She kept digging.

His face! She'd found his face. His beautiful, beloved, blue-lipped face.

Her arms kept digging, because they didn't yet know what her eyes already knew, what her heart refused to admit.

No.

He had to be alive. He had to be, because she'd *told* him she couldn't undo death, she'd been *very, very* clear on that point, and there was *no way* he would leave her, just up and die after a thousand lonely years of waiting for someone exactly like him to fill her heart fuller than she'd ever imagined it could be.

So of course he wasn't *dead*. He couldn't be dead because he was the other half of her soul and *she* was still alive, and fate would never be so cruel as to leave her alive and him dead, just minutes after he'd said *I love you*.

She should've said it back. She'd *meant* to say it back. She should've been the one to say it first, dammit. She should've said it over and over again until he was so tired of hearing about how much she loved him, he would've covered her with kisses and then made love to her.

Her eyes fell to his blue, blue lips.

There would be no kisses. Not anymore.

He wasn't breathing. Probably hadn't been breathing since the earth rose up around him.

She didn't want to think about that, didn't want to think about anything, except maybe the earth rising up to swallow her, too. She wouldn't mind not breathing. It would be much better than continuing on for eternity with a despair so deep it felt like the lightning-crusted sky had ripped out her very soul.

"Seventy," she whispered brokenly. "You were supposed to live to be *seventy*."

And it was her fault he hadn't.

She'd made a choice. She'd chosen saving the bus over saving him, and now he was gone and he wasn't coming back and she'd never even gotten to say *I love you* even though she'd been thinking it forever.

Her head was spinning, her breaths coming much too fast. But she couldn't stop digging his lifeless body out of the muck. He didn't belong here. Not like this.

She'd *tried* to make him stay home. She'd tried so *hard*, dammit. And he— And he—

He'd said *I love you, too,* which meant he knew, he'd figured out on his own that she loved him too, but that didn't mean she hadn't wanted to *say* it, to have him *hear* her say it, now that she wasn't invisible anymore. Now that she was finally Sarah.

But it was too late. He wasn't Javier anymore.

He was gone.

She struggled to her feet but didn't bother shaking the dirt from her clothes and hair. She was going back home, back to headquarters, back to the Heavenly Council. She'd found her One True Love and she wasn't going to stand for all this *death do us part* crap, no thank you, not a good deal at all.

No one could undo death, not even the

Heavenly Council, but there were other choices besides languishing on for eternity, now that she'd known true love. If death was the final answer, then let it be hers, too. So be it. But first, she had some choice words to share with the Council. A threat. And a promise.

She would make them an offer they couldn't refuse.

CHAPTER 15

Her wings shaking with grief and anger, Sarah took to the skies and flew straight toward the Governing Council of Heavenly Beings.

When she crossed the first barrier, Nether-Netherland stretched out in all directions. Its familiarity did little to calm her fears. Colorful tents and glittering poofs of pixie dust indicated the bimonthly bazaar underway. Disgruntled genies picketed for freedom in front of bored riot trolls. Flying horses soared high overhead.

In other words, her homeland was exactly the same as every other month, the same as when she first left a thousand years earlier. For all its magic and miracles, Nether-Netherland followed an archaic set of unforgiving rules, and those rules rarely bent for anyone. Sarah fully recognized how difficult it was going to be for her to change the minds of immortal angels. If effecting change were easy, djinns would have their freedom and working for transportation services wouldn't be synonymous with "pack animal."

But it didn't matter. She still had to try.

She touched down on the marble steps to the Governing Council's floating palace and slipped in through the front door. An immense antechamber filled with endless rows of waiting supplicants faded into seeming infinity. There was no other choice but to sit and wait. The Council didn't take appointments or offer a numbered ticketing system. They knew each angel was there as soon as he or she walked in the door, and they heard each case in whichever order they chose.

None of which made waiting any easier. Especially if the waiting took years. Or centuries.

In some ways, Sarah supposed she had it better than Nether-Netherland's non-angelic citizens, who fought drawn-out legal battles in courts of law with prosecutors and judges and government-appointed legal counsel. Instead of wasting time with gathering evidence and presenting testimony and hand-picking a jury of their peers, angels simply went before the Tribunal, whose word was the final say.

Then again, she supposed there was something to be said for due process. This would be her voice alone against the three highest-ranking angels in the heavens. That is, if she ever got the chance to speak. She half-suspected the Tribunal's strategy was to keep claimants on ice in the waiting area until they'd completely forgotten whatever it was that—

"Sarah Phimm, level two. Miss Phimm, please report to level two."

Sarah leapt to her feet, her heart thundering. She'd barely touched her feathers to an empty seat before her name was called. Disconcerted, she made her way to the second level. Maybe this was a sign. An indication that the Tribunal was open to alternate viewpoints, to hearing other perspectives. A harbinger of good things to come. She only wanted one thing: Javier. Maybe they were calling her so quickly because there was some loophole, some miracle the Governing Council could perform to make him whole and happy once again. Hope flooded her veins.

As soon as she reached the second level, her hopes plummeted.

Level two was a single vast chamber, so wide and so deep that its boundaries blurred into shadow, cold as a tomb, barren as the tundra. Not a place for miracles. The cavernous space was devoid of all decor, functional or otherwise, save for three tall pillars, upon which stood the three angels of the Tribunal:

Abram Junior, cofounder of the Heavenly Alliance of Guardian Angels.

Raphael, archangel and elected representative of the cherubim workers' union.

Dom, conductor of celestial virtues and presiding chief of the current Tribunal.

"Take a seat, Miss Phimm." Raphael's low voice boomed through the hollow emptiness and disappeared into the shadowy perimeter without so much as an echo.

Before the three white pillars was a small stone bench. Presumably, this was Sarah's assigned seat.

She sat.

Abram Junior was her boss's boss, in the sense that he governed over the principalities who managed the guardian angels' end-of-month debriefings. She'd vaguely realized he would've been receiving copies of all her monthly reports, but although she recognized him and the other angels from various industry holidays or Tribunal campaign buttons, this was the first time she'd ever come face-to-face with any of them.

She'd never felt smaller or more insignificant.

Partly due to the power play of the three of them literally standing upon high, while she hunkered down on a lowly stone bench. But mostly it was because, yikes. Raphael. Dom. Abram Junior. The three most powerful angels in all of Nether-Netherland and beyond.

She cleared her throat and tried to think of an opening line. One that would somehow simultaneously convey her awe and respect of them and their positions, while inoffensively (yet effectively) pointing out the need for immediate change and a reversal of—

"I presume you know why we've called this meeting." Dom's harshly angled face turned toward her, made all the more terrifying for its complete lack of expression.

Sarah swallowed. Crap. *They* had called this meeting? That meant they weren't remotely interested in her unsolicited advice and self-serving demands. Worse, that meant they wanted to talk about—

"Javier," she whispered.

Raphael inclined his golden-crowned head. "Yes. Javier Rodriguez. Your assignment."

She straightened her shoulders. "He's more than an assignment. He's my—"

"You were instructed to keep him safe and alive until his seventieth year," Dom reminded her coldly. "Is he safe, Miss Phimm? Or alive?"

Her heart clenched, and fresh tears clogged her throat. "No. He is not. Which is why—"

"Are you aware of the rule prohibiting guardian angels from appearing in physical form to their clients; visually, aurally, tangibly, or otherwise?"

"Yes, I—"

"Although perhaps not stated using detailed examples of every possible variation, did your comprehension of that rule include a correlated prohibition of interacting verbally, physically, and sexually with the assigned human under your protection?"

All three of them fixed her with penetrating stares.

"I..." Sarah's face flamed and her stomach churned. They didn't interrupt this time, though she fervently wished they would. This was not the direction she'd intended the conversation to go, and it was obvious by the phrasing of the question that the answer was already known and judgment had been passed.

"He's my one true love," she mumbled, then rose to her feet and stood tall upon the low stone bench. "He's my One True Love," she repeated loudly, confidently, letting the truth of the words condemn or absolve her as they may.

Rafael cocked a brow. "Do you think such a detail positions you above the law, Miss Phimm?"

"I *know* it does," she answered fiercely. "And so do you. Nothing in this world or any other has or shall have the authority to usurp or override true love."

Dom's smile was terrifying. "Are you saying the two of you were in love at the moment you first became visible to him?"

"Well... no. I—"

"Were the two of you in love at the moment you first began performing miracles that affected more than just your assigned client, thereby knowingly and willfully going against the rules you had sworn to uphold?"

"I don't know! Both the question and the situation are unfair." Her voice shook with anger. "Does the Council expect angels to stand idly by and let innocent children suffer simply because their names weren't assigned to a list?"

Raphael's blue eyes glittered. "Do you know *why* the Council only assigns one name per guardian angel, Miss Phimm?"

"Honestly?" Sarah's hands curled into fists. Why did they bother asking questions when her answers clearly didn't matter? They had no intention of changing, now or ever. She bit out, "I have no idea."

Abram Junior's low voice sliced through the resulting chill. "The rule is in place to enable guardian angels to stay focused. Fragmented focus is what causes mistakes."

"Mistakes like the death of assigned clients." Dom's expression was pointed. "Javier Rodriguez was under your protection, Miss Phimm. His death was *your* mistake."

"It was *not* a mistake," she replied softly. "True, I neither wanted nor chose for him to die, but nor could I allow a busload of children to fall to their deaths right in front of me. Saving their lives wasn't a mistake. It was a *choice*. One of the hardest I've ever had to face, but one that I deserved to be *able* to make."

Raphael smirked. "You value an individual snap judgment over the combined wisdom of the Governing Council of Heavenly Beings?"

Sarah's feathers trembled. "I value the lives of innocents more than I value bureaucracy, yes. Do you know what I've learned after nearly a millennium looking after humans?"

"Do tell us, Miss Phimm."

She straightened her spine. "Although their lives are but a blink compared to ours, the vast majority of them would give up every one of those paltry years in a heartbeat if it meant saving the life of someone they loved. Some humans, whether they be firefighters or preschool teachers or complete strangers, are willing to lay down their lives for people they don't even know, simply because they believe all life is precious. Are you saying the Governing Council believes otherwise? If *all* life is precious, then the rules are *wrong,* and it is past time for a change."

Rafael's smile was chilling. "You realize we cannot continue to allow you to operate as a guardian angel."

"I don't *want* to operate as a guardian angel!" She leapt to her feet. "Not if these are the constraints I'm working with. How am I supposed to feel like a bringer of miracles if I stand by and let others suffer? How can I live with myself for the rest of eternity, knowing there are countless lives I could've saved, but I didn't lift a finger to help simply because those names weren't assigned to my roster?"

"The rules—"

"To Hades with the rules!" Her wings unfurled in anger. "How can you imagine I would want to return to a life in this world or any other, having finally known true love and having it ripped from me moments later? Javier

Rodriguez might've been a mere human, alive for only a handful of decades, but he was a force to be reckoned with and an angel in his own right. He performed more miracles in a single day than the Governing Council has in the past year, and we're *all* the poorer for not having him with us. He was a better angel than any of y—"

"Careful, Miss Phimm." Dom's velvety tone was laced with warning. "This council has guarded humans since the moment of their existence. Don't you think we have a Grand Plan?"

"I think your plan sucks." Without waiting to be formally dismissed, she turned and stalked toward the exit.

Just as she reached the doorway, Abram Junior swooped down to block her path.

"What?" she demanded, not caring if he smote her for her insolence.

He did not. His eyes held... understanding? "Just a moment, Miss Phimm. Angels out in the field are not privy to the design from above. But we've been watching you." His gaze pinned her. "Why were you assigned to Mr. Rodriguez?"

"To keep him alive?" Her feathers ruffled. What kind of question was that? It was a guardian angel's sole responsibility.

"*Why* were you meant to keep him alive?"

"Because he had a 'destiny,'" she answered bitterly. "Something that made him more important than little children."

"What do you think his destiny *was*, Miss Phimm?" Abram Junior's voice was sharp, but his eyes kind. "Given the shortage of guardian angels."

She stared back at him in dawning comprehension. There *was* a Grand Plan. "To… help those children? As a human guardian angel?"

Abram Junior inclined his head. "Mr. Rodriguez would not have stopped with Bolivia. Between now and his seventieth year, he would have saved countless more lives than the Heavenly Alliance of Guardian Angels could look after on our own. *That* was his destiny."

And now he was gone. Thanks to Sarah.

"But… the children…" she stammered. "The bus would have… If I had been allowed to help others too, if Javier and I had been allowed to work *together* from the very start—"

Dom and Raphael swooped down to flank Abram. "Because of men like Mr. Rodriguez, the Governing Council has been convening to create zones of operation for teams of guardian angels, rather than individually assigned clients. The heads of each zone will need to be able to make hard decisions, and always keep human lives the utmost priority. You have passed the test."

"The… test?" she echoed in disbelief. "The past few decades was a *test?*"

"The past few centuries," Dom clarified. "It was your Renaissance work that made us think you were due for a reassignment."

Raphael conjured a clipboard. "How do you feel about operating in an advisory capacity, and perhaps heading up the recruitment division? With Mr. Rodriguez, of course."

"*What?*" she gasped. Or meant to gasp. Nothing had come out of her mouth, not even air.

Abram Junior's eyes almost smiled. "If my daughter hadn't fallen in love with a mortal, I might not have believed it possible. But no one of this world or any other can stand in the way of true love. You deserve to spend your life with yours. If you'll come with me, I'll take you to him now. We can discuss the changes to your benefits package on the way."

Sarah's heart beat so fast she was certain it would explode with joy and surprise and wonder. "B-benefits package?"

CHAPTER 16

Javier cracked his eyes open carefully, and immediately squeezed them back shut.

Light. Too much light. Impossible light. Blindingly bright, as if he were surrounded by stars, or had somehow fallen inside of one and managed to stay alive long enough to go half-blind.

Wait. Alive? *The sinkhole.* The landslide.

"Am I dead?" he croaked.

"Yup," came the suspiciously cheery reply, which sounded equally suspiciously as if it had come from Sarah.

A slight pressure to his palm indicated someone was holding his hand. He risked cracking his eyes back open, just a slit, just to see.

He smiled. Definitely Sarah.

With wings.

How the hell had she saved him? He

could've sworn it was all over. When the ground had disappeared beneath him and the tree had fallen on top, shattering his ribs with the force of—

His ribs. They felt fine. They actually didn't feel like anything, which was how they usually felt when they were fine.

His head didn't hurt, either.

He distinctly remembered taking a tree branch to the cranium, right before he'd gotten a lungful of mud instead of oxygen. But his head didn't hurt and his lungs weren't crushed and... He could wiggle his toes. How bad off could he be if he could wiggle his toes?

Dead, he reminded himself. That was pretty bad off. "Am I in Heaven?"

He expected an easy *yes* or *no* to that one, but it appeared to be a stumper. A heated discussion quickly arose around him.

"...Only on the technicality, but how far are we from the Palisade line?"

"...Okay, sure, it's a suburb, but if all the angels live in the same suburb, couldn't you agree that..."

"...But if *nobody* knows for certain, then you can't say that it's *not.* Am I right?"

That did it.

Javier opened his eyes.

He was immediately blinded by an overabundance of light, but within seconds, the dazzling brightness had given way to vague shapes, and the vague shapes shimmered into splotches of color, and the splotches of color finally sharpened into people. Three people.

Not people. *Angels.* All three of them had wings.

"I *am* in Heaven," he breathed in wonder.

"Well..." Sarah wiggled her hand in a so-so gesture. "We couldn't decide."

He squinted past her. "Who's 'we'? I mean, obviously not *we.* I know who 'we' are. I mean—"

"Him?" She gestured. "That's A.J. He was my boss's boss until yesterday, and now he's my regular boss. He's also the cofounder of the Heavenly Alliance of Guardian Angels. And no, he's not gassy, that's just how he looks. He doesn't smile much." Sarah gestured to her other side. "This is Arabella, his better half. She's the High Chair of the Fairy Godmother Committee, and kind of a big deal. If their daughter weren't an ex-tooth fairy, he might not have come to our rescue. Luckily, they've been down this road before."

Javier tried to make sense of that. Couldn't. Moved on. "I thought you were fired?"

"Well, I would've been. I mean, I was. I guess. On the other hand, it was more..."

"A lateral transfer," Arabella-the-fairy-godmother put in helpfully.

"Exactly," Sarah agreed. "Completely lateral. Finding my One True Love—that's you, if you weren't following—would've disqualified me anyway, even if witnesses hadn't seen me use the

Superman pose to fly the school bus to safety. I had to. It was iconic. Even if they've already forgotten."

Javier focused on the part he could understand. "DC Comics, issue number seven-oh-eight? The one with Diana?"

Sarah shook her head. "Superman the movie, circa 1978. The one with Christopher Reeve."

Arabella wrinkled her nose. "You can't pull off 'iconic' while wearing an elf costume."

"You weren't there," Sarah answered primly. "It was epic."

Javier waved a hand between them. "Wait a second. If you're not a guardian angel anymore, what are you? You still have wings."

Sarah and Arabella exchanged amused glances. A.J. remained expressionless.

"I'm a recruiter now," Sarah explained with obvious pride. "For the Governing Council of Heavenly Beings. It's *way* better than being a guardian angel. Er, sorry, A.J." She lowered her voice to a whisper. "But it totally is. I have business cards and he doesn't."

Javier was starting to feel drunk. "What does a heavenly recruiter even do?"

"Recruits people," she answered, as if it were the most obvious thing on earth. "The Heavenly Council has been working on a major restructuring for centuries. Instead of a one-to-one watcher-to-client ratio for guardian angels—which, as you yourself noticed, leads to uneven disbursement of miracle workers—the force is slowly being reallocated to *zones* instead of individuals. Just like tooth fairies!"

Javier could think of nothing to add to any of that. Instead, he asked, "When do you start?"

"I already did. We're assigned to Bolivia. But that's not the best part! They're not going to separate us. *Nothing* can separate true love. You're mine forever!"

He'd understood maybe two percent of anything she'd said so far, but *you're mine forever* was clear as crystal, and exceptionally good news. Even if he didn't quite grasp how it could be possible, it seemed like the sort of announcement that would deserve a kiss. He couldn't imagine how he'd even managed to go this long without kissing her. He leaned upright and reached out his arms...

And felt an unfamiliar pull at his shoulder blades as a pair of snow-white wings unfurled from his back.

"What. The. F—"

Sarah swooped in to kiss him. "None of that, babe. You're an angel now. Angels are pure of heart and soul and mouth." She lowered her lips to his ear. "Just kidding. You can talk to me as dirty as you want as soon as my boss is out of earshot."

"I'm an *angel*?" He was so dumbfounded, he could barely speak. "All this is really real? You're mine, forever?"

"Forever," she agreed with a sexy grin. "Till never ever do us part."

He pulled her into his arms and held her so tight he was afraid he would break her. But she wrapped her arms around him and squeezed back even harder, as if she, too, couldn't stand even a hairsbreadth of space between them, and an eternity of loving each other wouldn't be nearly enough time.

"I love you," she whispered fiercely. "I'm sorry I didn't say it fast enough before. I felt it, though. From the beginning. I've always, always loved you."

"I love you, too." He buried his face in her neck, horrified at the sudden sting at the edges of his eyes. "Is it okay for a brand new, very manly angel to cry a tiny bit, if it's tears of joy?"

She hiccup-laughed into his shoulder. "You can do whatever you want. It's Christmas!"

Christmas. He'd almost forgotten. It was time to celebrate it right.

Javier claimed Sarah's mouth with a highly unangelic kiss and then held her close to his heart, silently giving thanks to all the angels and fairy godmothers and Santa Clauses of the world for the most precious miracle of all.

True love.

THE END

~

THANK YOU FOR READING

Don't forget your free book!

Sign up at http://ridley.vip for members-only exclusives, including advance notice of pre-orders, as well as contests, giveaways, freebies, and 99¢ deals!

~

Check out the official website for sneak peeks and more:
www.EricaRidley.com/books

In order, the *Magic & Mayhem* books are:

Kissed by Magic
Must Love Magic
Smitten by Magic

In order, the *Gothic Love Stories* are:

Too Wicked to Kiss
Too Sinful to Deny
Too Tempting to Resist
Too Wanton to Wed

In order, the *12 Dukes of Christmas*:

Once Upon a Duke
Kiss of a Duke
Wish Upon a Duke
Never Say Duke
Dukes, Actually
The Duke's Bride
The Duke's Embrace
The Duke's Desire
Dawn With a Duke
One Night With a Duke
Ten Days With a Duke
Forever Your Duke

In order, the *Rogues to Riches* books are:

Lord of Chance
Lord of Pleasure
Lord of Night
Lord of Temptation
Lord of Secrets

Lord of Vice

In order, the *Dukes of War* books are:

The Viscount's Tempting Minx (FREE!)
The Earl's Defiant Wallflower
The Captain's Bluestocking Mistress
The Major's Faux Fiancée
The Brigadier's Runaway Bride
The Pirate's Tempting Stowaway
The Duke's Accidental Wife

Want to be the first to know about sales?

Follow me on Bookbub.

ACKNOWLEDGMENTS

As always, I could not have written this book without the invaluable support of my critique partners. Huge thanks go out to Darcy Burke, Emma Locke, and Erica Monroe. You are the best!

Lastly, I want to thank my *Historical Romance Book Club* and my fabulous street team. Your enthusiasm makes the romance happen.

Thank you so much!

ABOUT THE AUTHOR

Erica Ridley is a *New York Times* and *USA Today* best-selling author of paranormal romantic comedies and historical romance novels.

In the *12 Dukes of Christmas* series, enjoy witty, heartwarming Regency romps nestled in a picturesque snow-covered village. After all, nothing heats up a winter night quite like finding oneself in the arms of a duke!

Her two most popular series, the *Dukes of War* and *Rogues to Riches,* feature roguish peers and dashing war heroes who find love amongst the splendor and madness of Regency England.

When not reading or writing romances, Erica can be found riding camels in Africa, ziplining through rainforests in Central America, or getting hopelessly lost in the middle of Budapest.

~

Let's be friends! Find Erica on:
www.EricaRidley.com

Made in the USA
Middletown, DE
30 October 2023